CW00430324

Dear Reader

Welcome to Wilbu... ...
4,523, a town whe... ...y
the local diner or bar, which has the real
romantic action!

When three single men—FBI agent Max Riley,
billionaire Troy Cramer and playboy Jake
Malloy—suddenly find themselves daddies, the
employees of the Evans daycare centre come to
the rescue. But while sassy Caro, policewoman
Sadie and homespun Hannah teach these
DAYCARE DADS how to care for their
children, Max, Troy and Jake give a few
lessons of their own—lessons in love that
change the Evans girls' lives.

So, let's take a seat in the park—because it's on
a hill, and you can see most of the town from
any one of the benches—and watch as Caro
teaches Max everything from nappies to
discipline, and Max makes his points on the
fine art of seduction.

Happy reading!

Susan Meier

Susan Meier is one of eleven children, and though she has yet to write a book about a big family, many of her books explore the dynamics of 'unusual' family situations, such as large work 'families', bosses who behave like overprotective fathers, or 'sister' bonds created between friends. Because she has more than twenty nieces and nephews, children also are always popping up in her stories. Many of the funny scenes in her books are based on experiences raising her own children or interacting with her nieces and nephews. She was born and raised in western Pennsylvania, and continues to live in Pennsylvania.

BABY ON BOARD

BY
SUSAN MEIER

MILLS & BOON®

First published in Great Britain 2006
Harlequin Mills & Boon Limited,
Eton House, 18-24 Paradise Road, Richmond, Surrey TW9 1SR

© Linda Susan Meier 2003

ISBN 0 263 84894 9

Set in Times Roman 12¼ on 14¼ pt.
02-0406-52873

Printed and bound in Spain
by Litografia Rosés, S.A., Barcelona

Chapter One

It went without saying that any woman from Wilburn, Pennsylvania, over the age of twenty-five hated Max Riley.

Caro Evans was twenty-six.

Nonetheless, she followed him up the sidewalk of a Las Vegas, Nevada, home because he had contracted with her Aunt Sadie's day care for a representative to go with him when he picked up his six-month-old daughter from her maternal grandparents. Because Caro was an elementary-school teacher who spent summers training fathers in the single-dad school division of the day care, she was the perfect person for the task with Aunt Sadie unable to run the day care because of an illness. Caro had her teaching certificate, which maintained the day care's credibility. Plus, Aunt Sadie needed the money.

Max rang the bell and a slack-faced man who looked to be in his late fifties answered.

"Come in, Max. Who's your friend?"

As Max entered the foyer, he shook hands with their host. "This is Caro Evans. She works for a day care in Pennsylvania. Caro, this is Bill Russell."

Bill shook Caro's hand. "Nice to meet you."

"You, too," Caro murmured.

Max smiled ruefully. "I thought it best to have a pro with me. I'm not foolish enough to try to travel almost three thousand miles alone with a baby."

"Good thinking," Bill agreed.

Though the conversation came to an uncomfortable halt, Caro was too busy enjoying the air-conditioned foyer to care. Residents of the Appalachian Mountain town of Wilburn weren't accustomed to the three-digit temperatures of the desert in June, and in her shorts and lightweight top, Caro was baking. But even in jeans and a polo shirt Max Riley appeared oblivious to the heat.

Of course, he wasn't from Wilburn anymore. He and his parents left town the year he graduated from high school and Max now traveled around the country since becoming an FBI agent after law school. Tall and lean, blessed with shiny black hair, brilliant-blue eyes, a high IQ and street smarts that made him dangerous, Max Riley could have been lethal in the courtroom. It surprised most people when he chose the FBI. Caro thought the career fit him perfectly. Particularly since it kept him from returning home. He always seemed to be ''on assignment'' when his friends got married or at class reunion time.

''I'm really sorry about Linda,'' Max said, breaking the awkward silence. When Sadie had briefed Caro for this job, she explained that Max had at one time been involved with the Russells' daughter Linda, an FBI colleague, who had been killed in the line of duty the month before. Sadie also said that Max hadn't known he and Linda had a child together until he heard rumors from fellow agents who attended her funeral.

''Thanks,'' Bill said just as a short, pale woman appeared in the doorway behind him. She held a six-month old, who was dressed in a bright-pink sunsuit. Chubby and happy, the baby had a head of dark curls and breathtaking blue eyes. Obviously Max's child.

Caro said nothing. Did nothing. Even her facial expression didn't change. She was not a part of this drama. She was hired help.

"This is my wife, Alana," Bill said, introducing her to Caro.

"It's nice to meet you, Mrs. Russell."

Alana Russell nodded and attempted a smile, but she wasn't very successful. Her trembling lips rose only slightly. Caro understood why. The grief over the loss of her daughter the month before would still be fresh and raw. Giving up her granddaughter on top of that would be torture. But Max had told Caro's Aunt Sadie that the Russells couldn't keep Bethany. Both were up in years and Bill was about to undergo chemotherapy. His prognosis was good, but the Russells were wise enough to see they couldn't care for a baby with Bill's health in question.

Bill stretched out his arm so his wife could slip beneath it for comfort. "And the baby, of course, is Bethany."

Max nodded once. "Okay. What I think we should do is—" he began, but Alana interrupted him.

"Let's not talk in the foyer. Come into the living room. I'll get you something to drink and we can discuss everything…"

"At this point, there's nothing to discuss," Max said, his voice businesslike and neutral. "Linda and I were only dating for a short time. We weren't married. We weren't even living together. I don't know that's my child. I don't want to take Bethany and raise her as my own only to discover two years down the road that she belongs to somebody else. A friend of mine runs a lab in the area. I can make arrangements for him to do DNA tests and then we'll know for sure if I should take Bethany home.''

Alana looked stunned, but Bill jerked like a man who had been sucker punched. The slack jowls of his lower face firmed as he drew up his chin. His brown eyes narrowed. Caro could almost hear his teeth grind in fury. Before he spoke, he drew a short, control-inducing breath.

''Exactly what are you accusing Linda of?''

''I'm not accusing Linda of anything. I'm saying it's wiser for me not to get involved with a baby that isn't mine than to take this little girl to my house, expose her to my complete lack of child-care ability, and then discover she belongs to a secret lover.''

''You were Linda's lover at the time.''

Max conceded that with a nod. ''Yes, but I don't know that I was the only one.''

For thirty seconds Caro thought Bill would punch Max. Thick tension made it almost impossible to breathe. Even Caro's muscles quivered with indignation. In a cursory glance, any idiot could see that the baby belonged to Max. Only a fool or an insensitive clod would deny it. But this was vintage Max. And Caro wondered why she had been surprised that he was refusing to accept responsibility without proof. And not just any proof. DNA. Proof beyond a shadow of a doubt.

The creep.

If she didn't realize from looking at Bethany that the DNA test would bind Max to raising her, Caro would think he was going to desert another child. Just as he had left Caro's older sister's friend Mary Catherine Connor alone and pregnant fourteen years ago, and as a result had left Brett Connor fatherless, it appeared that Max was trying to leave Bethany Russell without a dad.

Alana raised her chin and looked Max in the eye. "How about if we make you wait for a court order for those tests of yours?"

Max smiled. "Whatever."

Caro struggled to hold back a gasp. It almost seemed that he was picking a fight with them…

Of course! Because Bethany was clearly Max's child, the only way he could get out of accepting responsibility for her would be to embroil the grandparents in a court battle. Then he wouldn't have to take Bethany until the trial and all the appeals were over.

Bill's face reddened with rage. "We'll get your

tests. You tell us when and where to have the baby and we'll be there. Now, get out.''

Max turned to the door. ''Once I make the arrangements with my friend, I'll call…''

''Have Caro call,'' Bill said, and Caro suddenly wondered about her real purpose for being along on this trip. This was supposed to be a simple assignment. Travel to Nevada with Max Riley, care for his baby overnight and on the long journey home, leave him at the door of his deceased grandfather's house on Farren Street, get a big fat check for Aunt Sadie, and, hopefully, never see him again. She hadn't questioned why she and Max had registered at a hotel before driving to the Russells'. She assumed part of her purpose was to care for Bethany until a flight out the next morning so they didn't have to travel cross-country twice in the same day. Now that she had surmised Max was trying to wiggle out of having to take Bethany, she suspected she was nothing but a decoy, a baby-sitter carted along so the Russells wouldn't guess what he was up to.

Plus, no one had said anything about Caro being a negotiator or a go-between.

Without another word, Max opened the door and stepped out into the oppressive heat. After one final glance at the furious grandparents and adorable Bethany, Caro scrambled after him.

"Are you nuts?" she asked, grabbing his arm to stop him as he strode toward the white car they had rented at the airport. "Or are you just a complete jerk?"

"Neither of those is any of your business," Max said as he shook off her hand, rounded the hood of the car and walked to the door. He opened it and jumped inside. Paying no attention to the fact that she was paralyzed on the sidewalk, gaping at him, he started the engine. Caro knew that unless she wanted to stand in the merciless Las Vegas sun all morning, she had no choice but to leap in beside him.

"They are my business," she corrected, glaring at him. "Especially since you alienated the Russells enough that I'm now your go-between."

"Sorry about that," he said without a hint of real remorse. "But making you a go-between wasn't my idea. If it makes you mad or you don't want to do it, you'll have to take it up with Bill."

Not sure what to do, Caro combed her fingers through her chin-length hair, closed her eyes and leaned back against the passenger-side seat of the car with a huff.

Max slowly let out the breath he had been holding. He hid the fact that his hands were shaking. He couldn't believe it. This baby really was his. Just looking at Bethany he could see he and the little girl shared the same genes. It had seemed as ridiculous to him as it had to Caro Evans that he insist on the DNA test, and he felt like the jerk she accused him of being for forcing the issue. But he also knew he had no choice.

So, he wouldn't let himself think any further ahead than his next step, which was to call his friend and make arrangements for the DNA test.

But as he drove to the hotel, his thoughts and his gaze drifted to the right, to the woman who was obviously furious with him, and he felt an unexpected tug of regret for making her dislike him more than she already did. Average height and weight, with round eyes the color of coffee, and blond hair, Caro Evans had the kind of natural beauty most women could only dream about. He would bet a full year's salary she didn't wear makeup, because she wouldn't have to. Her skin was clear and creamy, a shade of pink and ivory that couldn't be manufactured. She had long brown-black eyelashes with no telltale smudges of additives. Not seeing a dark line at the roots of her hair, or even the hint of one, Max would also bet the rich yellow hue was her own and not a color she'd chosen from a beautician's chart.

Still, he didn't regret using her because she was attractive, or even because she was the little sister of one of his high-school friends, Luke Evans. He

felt odd about dragging her through this mess with
him and the Russells because she was nice. He
had thought he was immune to nice. He really did.
But there was something about Caro Evans's
brand of nice that got to him. She hadn't done
anything overt like help lost children find their
parents at the airport that morning. It was more
that she smiled at people, joked with airport employees, and hadn't once seemed offended at being in his company. A few times she had been
downright accommodating.

Until now.

"Here you go," Max said when he parked the
car under the portico of the hotel. He had decided
to drive to the lab rather than call Jack Franklin,
because once he phoned his friend he would have
nothing to do for the rest of the day. Then he and
Caro Evans would be together but alone in this
wonderful hotel, a hedonistic playground specifically designed for entertainment. He wouldn't
have chosen this establishment if he had made the
reservations himself, but Caro's Aunt Sadie had
demanded to use her own travel agent. For her
employee's safety, she had said. And Max had
agreed. But the truth was, Sadie's travel agent had
gotten Max a real deal on both the airline tickets
and the hotel. And Max knew Sadie had done this
for him because she was one of the very few peo-

ple in his former hometown of Wilburn who didn't hate him.

Unfortunately that meant he and Caro were staying in a casino—a sensual, noisy, nothing-but-fun casino—and because she was so sweet, he had actually wished, when they'd checked in, that they had come to Las Vegas for a holiday, not to pick up a baby. But he had given up on dating, being friends with or even associating with anyone from Wilburn a long time ago.

Though it wasn't quite second nature to quash his impulses toward Caro Evans the way it usually was with the other town residents, he did it anyway.

"Rather than call," he told her now, "I've decided to go to the lab office to make the arrangements for the DNA test. I'll phone you once everything's confirmed, and you can call Bill. I probably won't get back in time for lunch, so either charge it to your room or keep your receipt. I'll reimburse you."

Caro only nodded and jumped out of the car. She virtually ran through the dark double-doored hotel entrance when it opened for her.

Max wasn't a hundred percent sure why, but he stared after her. He watched the way she walked, enjoyed the feminine symmetry of her body, and only when she was completely gone from view did he drive away.

Max called Caro that afternoon and she in turn called the Russells to tell them the time Max had arranged to meet at the lab to take the DNA samples the next day. After that, she easily amused herself gambling and sightseeing. When she returned to her room, arms laden with souvenirs and a coin cup for her sparse winnings, she was amazed to discover it was five o'clock—eight o'clock in Wilburn with the time difference—and she hadn't eaten dinner.

Sitting on the edge of her bed, and without giving herself a chance to think it through, she dialed the number for Max Riley's room. Not because she regretted her near confrontation with him that morning and wanted to apologize, but because she was here to work. Though it was true he didn't require her services until he had physical custody of the baby, and probably also true that they wouldn't be taking the baby home this trip, she and Max needed to talk about what they would do the next day.

When he answered, he sounded as if she had awakened him.

"I'm sorry, Max, if I woke you, but I was about to go downstairs for dinner, and thought if you hadn't yet eaten we could have supper together and discuss our plans for tomorrow.''

He cleared his throat. ''I haven't eaten, but there's nothing for us to talk about. I'll go into Jack's lab the same time the Russells take Bethany so everybody is assured the appropriate controls are in place on the samples. Then we're clear until Jack gets the results. Depending upon his workload, we might be here another day or two.''

''Oh.''

''Does that bother you?''

Not when he was paying Aunt Sadie double the usual hourly rate for twenty-four hours a day since Caro was forced to be out of town twenty-four hours a day. They had rooms on different floors so she didn't even run into him by accident. Her time was her own. And she was seeing a city she might have never seen had he not hired her.

''No, I'm fine. But I'm guessing this means I can go eat on my own then.''

''Yes.''

''You're sure?'' she asked politely, careful to put sincerity in her voice because she wanted him to realize that what he decided to do with his child, how he behaved, and even who he was, meant nothing to her. She had slipped up that morning when she'd become angry with him, but that was because she was worried she was becom-

ing a go-between. Now that her one phone call to
Bill Russell had been made and that end of her
job was done, she would go back to being completely neutral, because being neutral was the only
way to treat a Max Riley.

He, her brother Luke, Rory Brennan and Jake
Malloy had been the high-school jocks when Caro
was twelve. She knew all about their antics because her two older sisters, Maria, Mary Catherine's best friend, and Sadie Junior, named after
their dad's youngest sister, and their friends had
talked incessantly about the quartet of hellions.
The boys had loved getting away with little
pranks like stealing apples from Tilly's and gluing
condoms to the principal's car. They were on the
football team that won the state championship, so
no one would punish them because they were he-
roes. They would be called in and get yelled at,
but they would never be punished. For the years
they were the cornerstone of the best football
team in the state they had a power of sorts. As
long as they didn't cross the line into real crime
or violence, they could pretty much do as they
pleased. *That* was what they loved most of all.

So today, fourteen years later, Caro wouldn't
give Max the satisfaction of thinking she had an
opinion about what he did. She wouldn't even
give him the satisfaction of disliking him.

"I'm…" He paused. "Actually, I'm hungry."

"Then have dinner with me," Caro said matter-of-factly.

He paused again before he said, "Okay."

Caro suggested they meet in front of a small shop that was something like a convenience store where hotel guests could buy everything from sunscreen to hard liquor. Across from the convenience store was a boutique. Beside that sat a jewelry store. Three restaurants were strategically placed between the boutique and shops. At the end of the hall was a wedding chapel.

"Isn't this amazing?" she asked Max as he approached her. He had changed from his polo shirt and jeans and now wore trousers and a short-sleeved dress shirt. As always when she looked into his stunning blue eyes, she felt a jolt of recognition of how attractive he was, but she was fairly certain a woman would have to be dead not to feel something when she got within ten feet of him. She was smart enough to dismiss what she felt as a typical biological reaction. Knowing that he had left Mary Catherine Connor alone and pregnant, Caro had absolutely no fear that she would fall for this guy. Not for his looks. Not for his lines.

"What's amazing? The hotel?"

"It has everything!" Caro said, then directed

him toward the Italian restaurant, which wasn't as loud and crowded as the buffet or as expensive as the establishment that boasted a French chef.

"You like Italian food?"

"I love all pasta," she said as they waited for the hostess.

"You didn't have to pick the cheapest place. I'm not exactly poor."

"I didn't pick the cheapest place. I chose the middle place. And I don't care how much money you have."

Max laughed. "Well, that's certainly getting all our cards on the table."

"Ah, a gambling metaphor," Caro said, changing the subject with a little humor because she had slipped again. Telling him she didn't care about his money was like admitting she disliked him, which was bad because it gave him an opening to talk about himself. Unfortunately, even as she had that thought she also realized that if she didn't let him talk about himself and she refused to reveal anything about herself, they wouldn't have dinner conversation. "I guess a gambling metaphor is appropriate since we're in Vegas."

The hostess arrived, they were led to a private table, and problem number two reared its ugly head. Caro tried to ignore the dimly lit room and pretend she didn't notice the romantic atmosphere, but the farther into the restaurant they walked, the clearer it became that it was probably a haven for honeymooners.

Apprehension tightened her nerves. Not only had she chosen this place, which might give Max all kinds of wrong ideas, but also, if they didn't speak, they would be gazing at each other over a fat white candle. A violinist would probably serenade them.

As she sat, Caro desperately tried to think of something funny to say about her choice of restaurant and how it didn't reflect anything but her desire for spaghetti, but she came up empty.

Max leaned against his chair's broad velvet back and glanced around. ''This is nice.''

Caro cleared her throat. ''Yeah, it's great,'' she said, almost dropping her fork when she nervously picked it up to give herself something to look at other than him.

Though the next thirty seconds were quiet, Caro didn't as much as venture a peek in his direction. Not even to see if she could figure out what he was thinking—because she didn't want to know. She had chosen one of the most romantic restaurants in the city to have dinner with her town's most disreputable former citizen.

She was an idiot.

"So," Max said, breaking the oppressive silence. "What's it like to be a teacher?"

Caro's breath almost whooshed out of her lungs in relief, but she caught it just in time. Grateful he either hadn't gotten the wrong idea or didn't intend to capitalize on her mistake, Caro decided her life was dull enough that she wouldn't sweep him off his feet or fill him with unspeakable desire if she revealed a few tidbits. "What do you want to know?"

He shrugged. "Tell me anything. Keep me awake long enough to eat."

"You didn't sleep last night?"

He shook his head. "Not really."

Little pinpricks of recognition skittered up her arms. Whether Max intended to or not, he had presented her with an opportunity to confront him about leaving Mary Catherine by asking him why he hadn't slept. She knew the answer would be something about Bethany, and talking about Bethany would lead to discussing the similar situation with Brett Connor. And once he mentioned Brett it was only a short jump to a chance to confront him about Mary Catherine.

But she didn't want to know his reasons for leaving Mary Catherine. She really didn't. Her sisters did. Her brother probably did. And her parents might, but she didn't.

She said only a noncommittal, "That's too bad."

"Right," Max said, then sighed with disgust. "Come on, Caro, let's cut the bull or we're going to have the most miserable dinner in recorded history. You're dying to yell at me about the DNA test, so let's just get it over with."

Caro only stared at him, puzzled because she really didn't give a darn about the DNA test. She had already decided that his trying to wiggle out of caring for Bethany was merely an extension of his typical behavior. The uninvited question that kept popping into her head was how he could desert Mary Catherine and never tell anybody why. And not only was that answer none of her business, *he* was none of her business. Everything about him was none of her business.

"I don't want to yell at you. You and your paternity accusations aren't my concern."

"This isn't an accusation. I know Bethany is my baby."

Confused again, she gaped at him. "Then why are you demanding tests?"

"For the Russells."

This time her face scrunched up in confusion. "Huh?"

"Think about it. In three months, when the grief of losing their daughter begins to abate, they

are going to realize they gave their only grandchild to a virtual stranger. More than that, they
are going to realize Linda never told me about the
baby and they are going to wonder about her reasons. Then they're going to try to get Bethany
back.''

''And with your DNA proof, they won't have
a leg to stand on?''

Max toyed with his silverware. ''It's more than
that. What I'm doing is forcing them to go
through all the emotions right now of disliking
me, mistrusting me and fearing for Bethany, and
then get beyond that to the point that they see my
raising Bethany is for the best. I want them
through all this to become comfortable with me
before I take Bethany three thousand miles
away.''

Because that plan could actually be construed
as considerate of the Russells, and Caro didn't
believe he was considerate of anyone, she stared
at him. ''Don't try to tell me you were blunt with
the Russells for their own good.''

He peeked up at her. ''Why is that so hard to
believe?''

''Because you were rude!''

He shrugged. ''I had to be rude. I had to force
them to face the issues. I had to force them to
acknowledge and accept that they were giving up

their baby permanently because there isn't going to be any turning back from this.'' He drew a quick breath. ''That's what the DNA test was all about.''

''You weren't trying to wiggle out of paternity?'' Caro asked skeptically. ''Or buy yourself some time?''

He laughed. ''Bill Russell will be starting chemotherapy next week. I can't buy time. We don't have time. And that's the whole point. I have to take Bethany now. The Russells have to accept the situation.''

''And you figured casting aspersions on their daughter was the best way to get them to accept you?''

''I didn't cast aspersions on Linda. I made myself look mean.''

''And I'm sure that will give them comfort when they wake up the morning after you've taken Bethany and realize they've given their granddaughter to a man who is mean.''

''No, it will give them comfort when they wake up and realize they've given their granddaughter to her real father and that there's no point in filing for custody because most courts will give a child to a natural parent over a grandparent. It will give them the basis to start accepting things.''

''It still seems counterproductive. I don't see

how you're going to get them to see you as the right person to raise their granddaughter by being rude.''

''Because I forced them to face some hard truths, this is all going to sink in for the Russells quickly. Then, after they've accepted that I'll be the one raising Bethany, I'll offer them liberal visitation, and they'll remember I wasn't such a bad guy in the few months I dated their daughter. And we'll start building our relationship honestly, openly, and with no fear of each other's motives. Because everything really is out on the table now.''

Caro frowned. His plan was unusual, but typical logic probably wouldn't have worked, particularly since their time was so limited. She hated to admit it, but his strange plan now sounded very good. Very logical. Still, it was hard to believe that the man who had gotten Mary Catherine Connor pregnant and then left town without so much as a backward glance or a care for how she would raise a baby on her own, had been sensitive enough to create a plan to help Linda Russell's parents. Max hadn't cared for Mary Catherine, yet he expected Caro to believe that fourteen years later in a similar situation he was going out of his way to help the grandparents of his baby in order that he could keep the baby.

"Oh, I get it," she said, realizing his tactic wasn't as benevolent to the Russells as it was convenient for him. "You're making them mad enough now to prevent having to deal with hysterics later."

He peered at her over the candle. "In a way, because I do want them to see that it's futile to file for custody. But I'm also trying to save the Russells a lot of heartache. Think of what I did as something like yanking a bandage off a cut. It hurts like hell at first, but it hurts less than the long, drawn-out process. I don't want them to hurt. I don't want any of us to hurt. I want us all to get along."

He meant that. Caro could hear it in the tone of his voice, see it in the expression in his sincere blue eyes. He had not been blunt and brusque with the Russells to help himself, but to force the Russells to accept this situation quickly and with the least amount of pain so that everyone could move on. The wisdom of forcing them through the emotions impressed her, but the fact that he had thought ahead to recognize they would need help and devised a plan to assist them touched her in a way she didn't want to be touched. Not by Max Riley. She didn't want to see Max Riley as a nice guy. Yet, he had recognized the need to help his baby's grandparents through a very difficult transition and that made it very hard not to at least consider the possibility that he wasn't the horrible person everybody in Wilburn made him out to be.

Or maybe that he had grown up.

The waitress arrived with menus, and they spent the next few minutes choosing their meals. But that was good, because by the time they had ordered, Caro had her perspective back. All she had to do was think of Mary Catherine, still unmarried, always struggling to make ends meet because she couldn't go to college the way Max had, and any possible kindness she might attribute to Max Riley was moot. Every good thing he did for the Russells was canceled out by the pain he'd inflicted on that poor woman.

When the waitress moved away from their table, Max picked up the conversation where he left off. "I think Linda didn't tell me she was pregnant because she wasn't sure she wanted to keep the baby."

Though Caro assumed he continued talking about this because he was looking for someone who could help him sort things through, as the baby sister of Mary Catherine's best friend, she didn't want to hear this. She fought to keep her expression neutral and to find a way to change the subject. None came.

Max didn't seem to notice she hadn't spoken and continued with his story. "From the timing, I would say Linda broke up with me the very second she suspected she might be pregnant. Then she got herself transferred to the FBI office here in Vegas and had the baby. Because of the physical distance between us, I never saw her."

In spite of not wanting any part of this conversation, Caro couldn't stop herself from asking, "Did you try?"

He smiled ruefully. "A few times. But she always said she was too busy to see me. We weren't really in a serious relationship. I mean, we dated. Off and on for years, actually, but neither one of us wanted to get married."

Not expecting anything different from Max Riley and knowing he had sucked her into a conversation she shouldn't be having, Caro only nodded. Apparently it had never crossed his mind that his not wanting to get married might have been the impetus to drive away his girlfriend when she suspected she was pregnant.

Still, that was none of Caro's concern. She was only here to help him take the baby home and she wasn't encouraging him to talk anymore. Not because he was swaying her opinion. He most certainly was not. Not even because he was making her mad. But because she wasn't about to give

him any more opportunities to explain himself or
make himself look different, better, than what she
knew him to be.

The waitress returned, bringing their drinks and
salads. As if the interruption had caused him to
finally figure out that she wasn't agreeing with
him, only nodding every once in a while, Max
asked Caro about herself when the waitress left.

"There's not much to tell. I'm an elementary-
school teacher who helps her aunt run her day
care in the summer when there are more kids."

"I thought enrollment was down at your aunt's
day care?"

Caro nodded. "It is." She took a bite of salad
and didn't elaborate because she knew her brother
probably had told him about Sadie's troubles
since Luke was the one who brought Max to Aunt
Sadie's day care. Luke had explained that Max
had returned to Wilburn two weeks before to clear
out his grandfather's house, which was for sale.
Gino Riley had died six months before, but Max's
parents had needed a few months to get accustomed to giving up the family home. The day
Max arrived in town he had called Luke and they
spent several evenings drinking beer on Max's
granddad's back porch. Then Max got the call
from the Russells' attorney, and he and Luke appeared at Sadie's day care.

At first, Caro had thought it was simply Max's connection to Luke that sent him to Aunt Sadie for help. Then she'd considered that Max might be doing Luke a favor by providing Sadie with the opportunity to earn so much cash. Now she recognized it was more the level of confidentiality he expected from his old friend's family that had caused him to choose Aunt Sadie's day care, when there were three others in Wilburn. The last thing he'd want would be for word to get out that he had another illegitimate child. Worse, it appeared he was taking responsibility for this one. She didn't know how this would play in a small town like Wilburn, but she suspected the reaction wouldn't be good. And Max was stuck at his grandfather's for another few weeks because the house wasn't anywhere near ready to turn over to a Realtor.

"So are you married, divorced, single…"

Max took her so much by surprise that Caro almost choked on her salad. "Excuse me?"

His blue eyes rose slowly, until he caught her gaze. "Are you married?"

Gazing into his stunning azure eyes, a sizzle of awareness shivered through Caro and she cursed it. She couldn't be attracted to this guy. He was a liar. He was a creep. He wasn't helping Sadie. He was protecting himself. He wasn't helping the

Russells, either. He might be saying that, but the same plan that pushed the Russells through a difficult situation also protected him. Everything Max Riley did, he did for himself.

She cleared her throat and pretended his question had little consequence—because it did. If he were the last man on earth. Caro wouldn't go out with him. Under normal circumstances, she wouldn't even speak to him.

"I'm single. And I'm probably going to stay that way forever," she added, not just to discourage him, but also because it was the truth. Thus far no relationship had been interesting enough or fulfilling enough to make her want to share the precious time she had for teaching. "Some days I feel like I'm raising twenty-five kids. That in and of itself satisfies my commitment and my maternal instincts."

"Does it bother you that you have to help raise other people's children?"

She looked him right in the eye. He of all people had a lot of nerve asking that question. First because he'd had little to no disciplining himself as a child. Second because he shirked the responsibility for his own son.

Nonetheless, Caro held her temper and answered honestly in the interest of keeping the conversation off Max, his children and his love life.

"No. Parents need all the help they can get these days. If more people took an active interest in the kids around them, like the kids they see at the park or their neighbors, we would have fewer juvenile delinquents."

"You mean fewer people like me."

There he went again! Presenting her with the chance to give him hell, level accusations, ask questions about what happened fourteen years ago. It was almost as if he wasn't letting her out of the restaurant until she kicked him but good for deserting Mary Catherine and Brett.

"No. I don't mean fewer people like you. You and my brother and your friends were bad because you enjoyed it. You liked the attention."

He smiled. "Yep."

Righteous indignation sputtered through her and her control deserted her. How dare he! How dare he be so flippant about the fact that he had ruined at least two lives. "And you think it's funny that you never had to take responsibility for Brett Connor?"

Only a fool would have missed the accusation in her tone and Max Riley had already proved he wasn't a fool. Though Caro had thought he was almost pushing her to talk about this, she saw his expression go from friendly to furious instantaneously.

"No. Actually, I don't. I don't think anything about that situation is funny." He rose, reached into his pocket and threw several bills on the table. "That'll cover dinner. I've changed my mind. I'm suddenly not hungry."

He walked away without another word and Caro's stomach clenched sickly. In her entire life she had never deliberately been rude to anybody, but she couldn't help it. He was arrogant, even smug, about getting away with leaving Mary Catherine…

Caro slumped in her seat. No. That wasn't true. As soon as he'd recognized that she was talking about his leaving Mary Catherine and not stealing pumpkins or any of the other pranklike things he and his friends had done, his entire demeanor had changed. His exit wasn't the exit of a smug man. It was the exit of an unhappy man. And now that she thought about it, that was the thing that had struck her oddly about Max Riley from the minute they began this trip. He wasn't happy. He hadn't walked away whistling fourteen years ago. He might have walked away, but he hadn't done so without regret, remorse or *something*.

He was a very unhappy man, and she, good, sweet person that she was reputed to be, had tormented him.

But the very second she internally voiced that

regret, another thought canceled it out. She had heard her older sisters talk a million times about how Max Riley was a hotshot Casanova with charm to spare. Mary Catherine, the smartest of their friends, had made the ''big'' mistake with him. Proving, her sisters theorized, that nobody was safe with him. Given enough private time, he could make anybody believe anything.

Could it be, Caro wondered, that Max Riley had just conned her?

Chapter Two

Two days later Max called Caro and told her to pack and meet him in the hotel lobby in an hour because they were heading home. She showered, dressed in a sleeveless white cotton blouse and orange capri pants and was at the registration desk in forty-five minutes. Max was already there. With the lights, bells and whistles of the casino in the background, he took her single blue-paisley suitcase from her and ushered her to the sliding glass door.

"I've checked us out of our rooms."

"Good," Caro said cheerfully, though she was about as confused as a person could be.

She hadn't seen him in the two days that had passed since their attempt at eating dinner together. Their only contact was a phone message in which he told her his friend had two unexpected rush jobs and wouldn't get to the DNA test until those were completed. He said he would contact her when it was time to leave, that she should save her receipts or charge everything to her room, and that he had authorized a hundred dollars a day for her for gambling. After apologizing for the delay, he told her he didn't want her to be bored, so the arrangements were made and she should simply have a good time until he called her.

That floored her. This was a man who wouldn't take responsibility for his son, yet he took responsibility for her being "stuck" in Las Vegas, and paid for her gambling so she wouldn't be bored.

It didn't make any sense.

She scampered after Max who took long-legged strides out into the oppressive heat. "So, are we going to the Russells'?"

Max handed his car keys to the valet. "Yep. The results are back. Bethany is mine. The Russells and I have talked several times by phone. They're ready for me to take her home. They understood my frankness with them and know they will be welcome anytime to see their granddaughter."

"That's important for them. So you made airline reservations?"

"Yes."

"Do you have the appropriate gear for the baby to travel?"

"The Russells are giving me all of Bethany's things."

Caro gaped at him. "Everything?"

"Well, everything we need to get home," Max replied casually. "They're going to parcel post the rest to my town house in Frederick, Maryland."

She couldn't tell from his tone if he was still angry with her, and didn't know if she cared, but the butterflies in her stomach clearly told her something was up. She felt something for him, though she shouldn't. First of all, she hardly knew him, but also, after he put his grandfather's house in the hands of a real estate agent, she would never see him again. So it didn't matter if she liked him or didn't like him. It also didn't matter if he liked her. But she had a fluttery feeling in her middle every time she was around him, and it wasn't always from guilt or confusion.

Max Riley was a very attractive man and she *wanted* to like him. But his looks were only part of his attractiveness. Very few people thought ahead to work through a situation the way Max

Riley had with both her and the Russells. And *that* was why she wanted to like him. She couldn't reconcile his past with his current behavior except to think that he had probably grown up. But that was good. Unless he was conning her and the Russells—and the jury was still out on that—the past fourteen years had changed him completely.

"Actually, while the Russells and I talk, I was hoping you could pack a bag for Bethany and gather up whatever we need."

Caro smiled briefly, ignoring the butterflies in her stomach, which seemed to increase their fluttering with every normal word he said to her. "Good."

The valet drove up with their white rental car. After he and Max loaded their two suitcases into the trunk, Max tipped him. Caro was already in the car waiting for him when he jumped inside, yanked the gearshift into drive and headed for the highway.

Neither one of them said a word for the entire thirty-minute trip to the Russells'. Max parked the car in front of their garage and got out. By the time he had rounded the hood, Caro was waiting for him by the sidewalk.

Seeing the apprehensive expression on his face, she let her typically kind nature supersede his reputation and even her own muddled feelings about him, and she smiled at him. ''Ready?''

He pressed his lips together and nodded. ''As ready as I'll ever be.''

They walked to the front door in complete silence. Max rang the bell. Again, Bill Russell admitted them into his home.

''This time we should go into the living room,'' he said softly, and Max followed him into the quiet room that was furnished with a sofa and love seat in dusty rose and beige print with cherry-wood accent tables.

As the trio entered from the foyer, Alana Russell entered the room from a door in the back, carrying Bethany. She stopped only a quarter of the way and Max took slow, cautious steps toward her and the baby.

''Can I hold her?'' he asked.

Alana nodded.

Max slid his hands around Bethany's middle and pulled the baby from her grandmother's arms. For a few seconds he held her in front of him, studying her face. Caro watched his eyes fill with unshed tears as he said, ''Hello, Bethany, I'm your daddy.''

The baby let out a resounding screech, and then she slapped him. With one chubby hand she gave Max four solid pats on the cheek. Had she not been happily gurgling "Goo" and "Ooooh" and "Ahhh" while she dribbled all over him, Caro might have gasped.

Max turned to Alana. "She's a happy little thing."

"Yes," Alana agreed. "She is."

Bill took several deep breaths, his barrel chest shivering as it expanded. Caro realized he was working very hard not to cry. "She's our only girl now."

Max continued to study the baby, blinking back the tears that kept accumulating in his eyes. "I almost can't believe this." He looked at Alana and smiled kindly. "She's as beautiful as Linda was."

Alana's lips trembled. "Yes, she is." She shook her head once and swallowed hard. "Linda used to complain bitterly that the baby looked like you, when *she* had done all the work. But I saw Linda in Bethany."

"I see her, too," Max whispered. He shifted the baby so she was lying on his arm. "Hello, Bethany," he said, tickling her chin. "We're going for a big ride. I'm going to take you to live with me."

"I don't think she understands," Alana said, then reached for a tissue on the table behind her.

Max glanced up to catch her gaze. "I don't

blame her. This is hard enough for the three of us to understand." He turned to Caro. "Caro, would you take the baby into the nursery and begin gathering her things while the Russells and I talk?"

Glad to get away, Caro nodded enthusiastically.

Alana faced her with a weak smile. "The room behind this one is the nursery. We had her in between our bedroom and the living room so we could listen for her while she napped. There are two diaper bags and a small suitcase. The diaper bags are packed with the things you'll need on the plane, like fresh diapers, a few bottles and toys. You can go through the rest of her things and pack what you think you'll need for the next few weeks. Better grab the safety seat, too, for both the car and the plane ride."

Caro reached for Bethany. The baby wiggled into her hands. Just as she had with Max, Bethany gleefully slapped Caro's cheeks. "Thanks, Mrs. Russell."

"You're welcome."

Bill offered Max a seat, and Caro slipped into the nursery. She set the gooing, clapping baby in her crib and glanced around. There were two dressers and an open closet full of clothes. The diaper bags sat to the right of the door and the suitcase was on the floor by the crib.

"Let's get you packed," she said to Bethany, who clapped and blew spit bubbles in response.

"Oh, you are cute," she said, lightly pinching Bethany's cheek. She bent over the rail of the crib and whispered, "But I think your mommy was right. You look just like your dad." She smiled at the baby, and, moving closer, added, "But that's actually a very, very good thing. You will thank him for those blue eyes when you're a teenager."

The baby screeched with delight and Caro laughed. She gave Bethany a teething ring and reached for the empty suitcase. She set it on the changing table and opened it.

Turning toward the first dresser to begin selecting clothes to pack, she heard Max say, "I don't know how to make this easier."

"No matter what you do, Max, this is going to be hard," Bill said. The shudder in his voice clearly indicated he was crying. But, also, Caro realized from the easy conversation that Max had really smoothed things over between them.

"If there was another way, I wouldn't take her."

Alana jumped on that comment like a lifeline. "You know we would be happy to raise her once Bill's treatment is complete."

"But then she would be over two thousand

miles away from her dad. Alana, I know what you're saying, and I appreciate your offer. But I think my raising her is the right thing.''

Caro opened the dresser drawer. *Damn it.* She wished she couldn't hear them. She wished she couldn't hear Max Riley once again confirming good things about himself, because she wasn't supposed to like him. Hell, she wasn't *allowed* to like him! Her sisters would skin her alive.

She set a stack of pajamas in the suitcase as Max continued speaking. ''My mother and I have talked about visits for you. You would be more than welcome at my town house, of course, but also my parents thought it might work for you to come down to Orlando and spend time with Bethany there, with them. You could go to Walt Disney World and have the kind of visits that would make memories.''

''That's very nice of them.''

''And, of course, we'll make arrangements for Bethany to come here. The only problem is that I won't always be able to bring her to you.''

''We'll be happy to fly to you to bring her home for a few weeks at a time,'' Alana quickly assured him. ''That's no problem.''

''That would work out really well,'' Max said through a relieved sigh. ''And, of course, my mother has been lecturing me about taking lots of pictures and getting a camcorder so I can video-tape all of her firsts.''

Caro busied herself with sorting through Beth-any's clothes. She diligently looked for dresses, T-shirts, jeans and tiny shoes. She concentrated on varying casual and dress clothes because she wanted to block out the living-room conversation. Her heart broke for the Russells, but Max did nothing but confuse her. He wasn't hell-bent on taking the child for spite or revenge or even be-cause he was doing his duty. He *wanted* this little girl. Caro could hear it in his voice. Yet, even if he had grown up in the past fourteen years, he had never once contacted Mary Catherine about Brett.

The conversation with the Russells lasted about half an hour. Caro stalled as long as she could before she knew it would become obvious that she was deliberately taking longer than necessary. As quietly as possible she brought the suitcase and safety seat to the living-room doorway, then slipped back into the nursery. When she returned with the diaper bags and Bethany—who was now wearing a sunbonnet and was liberally slathered with sunscreen—Max rose. Caro handed him the baby, then slid the diaper bags to his free shoulder.

Looking apologetically at the Russells, he said, "I'm sorry, but we have to go."

Bill nodded. After he pushed himself up from the sofa, he extended his hand to help his sobbing wife rise. Max gave Bethany to her and Alana held her tightly, whispering endearments and saying goodbye. Caro bit the inside of her cheek to keep from weeping, too. Max swallowed and looked away. Bill took the baby, hugged her, promised to visit, promised to call, and then broke down.

Max slid Bethany from Bill's arms and nodded in the direction of the foyer, indicating they should leave. Caro grabbed the suitcase and the lightweight infant seat and walked behind him toward the door.

He opened it, paused, then turned and said, "I'll call you when we arrive in Pennsylvania. I'll call you every week."

With that he turned and strode out of the house and down the sidewalk. When he reached the car, he rummaged through his pocket, found the keys and tossed them to Caro. "Here. You're driving."

Caro only nodded. She put the safety seat on the concrete driveway beside the car. Max opened the back door and tossed the two diaper bags inside. With Bethany on the crook of his arm, he grabbed the infant seat and slid it into place, while

Caro opened the trunk and shoved in Bethany's suitcase. By the time she had everything stowed away, Max had the car seat installed.

"How did you know how to do that?"

"You're not going to believe this," he said, putting Bethany in the protective carrier, "but I went to a department store and got a demonstration."

Caro laughed. "No kidding."

"Hey, I am out of my league here and way over my head. I've faced down people who wanted to shoot me. I once went undercover in a drug ring. But nothing ever stopped me dead in my tracks like the knowledge that I had to raise a little girl." He caught Caro's gaze. "Alone. I have to care for a baby by myself."

Caro smiled and nodded her understanding. But when he returned his attention to the car seat, her face scrunched up in confusion and she studied the top of his head. He acted as if this was his first child, and she supposed in some ways it was. Max could consider Brett Connor as a mistake of his youth, and in that convoluted logic find reason to ignore his son. But he didn't act like a man who was ignoring a child. From everything he had done in the past few days, she would also guess he wasn't a man who could walk away from a responsibility. And even if immaturity was the reason he'd left Mary Catherine fourteen years ago, now that he was an adult, shouldn't he get in touch with her, meet Brett and take responsibility for him?

"How does this look?" he asked, yanking Caro back to the present.

"Perfect," she said. "Like it was done by a pro."

He breathed a deep sigh of relief. "I'm gonna get this."

She nodded. "I know."

He slid into the passenger side and Caro got behind the steering wheel, turned the key in the ignition and pulled the gearshift into reverse. "I think I remember the way to the airport, but feel free to shout out the directions."

"Okay," Max said, but he stopped abruptly. Alana Russell was rushing toward the car. Caro shoved the gearshift back into park and Max lowered his window.

"This is her favorite stuffed toy," Alana said, tears streaming down her face as she passed a pink rabbit to Max. "She won't sleep without Mr. Bunny."

Nearly overcome by the woman's grief, Caro pressed her lips together. Max said, "Thanks."

Alana nodded. "Goodbye, Bethany," she said, and as if Bethany finally caught on to what was happening, she began to cry. "You better go," Alana said. She bit her bottom lip then whispered, "Bye, Beth."

Max quickly pressed the button to reposition the window. "Go," he said to Caro, who yanked the gearshift into reverse and backed out of the driveway.

Bill and Alana stood on the sidewalk waving, and as Caro drove down the street, she could see in the rearview mirror that they remained there, waving, until Caro turned the corner.

Max scrubbed his hand across his mouth. "Damn it, that was hard," he said before shifting on his seat to face Bethany. "What's the matter, honey?"

"Give her the bunny," Caro said, nodding at the pink satin toy Alana had given to Max.

"Oh, right," Max said as if he had forgotten he even held it. Caro didn't blame him. Seeing Alana's grief was enough to traumatize anyone. "Here you go. Here's…"

"Mr. Bunny," Caro supplied.

"Here's Mr. Bunny," Max singsonged. The baby only cried harder.

"Oh, boy," Max said, and Caro half laughed.

"Welcome to the real world of babies."

"What do we do?"

"Well, you just keep trying to entertain her

while I drive. The truth is, Max, she has to get accustomed to you. The more things you do with and for her the sooner she will trust you and the sooner she will be relaxed with you.''

''Makes sense.'' Max wiggled the bunny in front of the baby again. ''Here, Bethany. See Mr. Bunny dancing?''

Caro burst out laughing.

Max stopped and stared at her. ''A dancing bunny isn't good?'' he asked seriously.

''No. No. The dancing bunny is great.'' Caro eased the car onto the highway. ''See, she's even starting to settle down some, aren't you, Bethany?'' she said, looking at the sniffing baby in the rearview mirror. ''It's just a little odd seeing you making the bunny dance.''

''If you had a camcorder now, you could probably get good money for a video of this at FBI headquarters.''

''I'll bet I could,'' Caro said, realizing that they had again fallen into the comfortable rapport they had had naturally on the plane ride to Vegas. Though their getting along had mostly been a professional courtesy on her part, she knew that if she let herself, she could be totally comfortable with him, and she decided to relax and let nature take its course. She was here to help him, and though no one had specifically said she was to teach him, showing him how to deal with Bethany was better value for his dollar than taking care of the baby for him. Also, though, she finally figured out that part of the odd feeling she had in her stomach every time he was around was a sense of trespassing into an area where she didn't belong. She had been hired to help him on this trip home. She had not been hired to judge him.

From here on out, she was at his disposal for anything and everything he needed. Then she would earn her money, then she could leave him with a clear conscience. Much clearer than the conscience that had been nagging her for the past two days.

"So, how do you intend to go about finding a nanny?" she asked, speeding along the highway as Bethany chewed on the ears of her bunny and Max faced the back seat watching every move she made.

"There are services in D.C. that do that kind of thing. A few people at the Bureau have working wives who've hired nannies. I have resources."

"Good for you," Caro said, congratulating him because it was clear he had thought this through and right now he needed positive reinforcement.

"I haven't yet bought furniture for her bedroom. The walls are still white. The carpeting is beige. I have no clue about childproofing my town house," he said, ticking things off on his fingers. "But I'm hoping the nanny I hire will at least be able to help me with some of that."

"Probably," Caro said when he fell silent. "You may not know what to do, but as long as you find someone who does and you're open-minded about learning, you can get through this." She paused to glance at him. "Actually, if you really invest some time and energy into parenting, you could end up a darned good dad."

"I hope so," Max said, flopping back on the seat because Bethany had settled down.

When they arrived at the airport, Max took Bethany, car seat and all, from the back seat. After stacking their suitcases and Bethany's diaper bags on the sidewalk with Max and the baby, Caro left them at the curb and drove the car to the rental drop-off. As she walked toward them after returning the car, she saw that Max was clearly a nervous wreck.

Continuing to be enthusiastic to help ease him into his new role, she said, "Look how well we travel. It doesn't have to be a problem to take a baby. You just have to pack right."

"Yeah," Max said, lifting the little girl in her car seat and hefting both of Bethany's diaper bags onto his shoulder before he turned toward the check-in for their airline. "Right."

"Once we leave our luggage at the desk," Caro said, nodding to Max's suitcase, which she rolled behind her, her suitcase on her shoulder and Bethany's in her free hand, "I'll take the diaper bags and you'll just have the baby."

"So what you're telling me is that in the future when Bethany and I fly, I don't get a carry-on bag."

"What I'm telling you is that your diaper bags become your carry-on," Caro said with a laugh.

"Got it."

"Good."

As they waited in line to check in, Bethany began to cry again. Max had no choice but to take her out of the safety seat and cuddle her. As Caro kicked the seat up the aisle, she dragged all three of their suitcases and the diaper bags. Then Caro held Bethany while Max pulled out his ID. Max held the baby while Caro dug out her ID. When their bags were checked and they had gone through security, they were left with only two diaper bags, one car seat and one baby.

"I still think this is a two-person job," Max mumbled as they strode down the airport concourse toward their gate. Walls of windows allowed passengers to see the flat desert runways in front of a wall of mountains. The noise of people flowed around them. Tired from crying, Bethany slept nestled against Max's shoulder as Caro hustled beside him lugging the two diaper bags and the infant seat. "If you weren't here I would either have to abandon the car seat or carry it on my head."

Caro laughed. "It's not that bad. You would think of something."

"I doubt it," Max said. "I can't imagine why Linda chose to keep me out of this," he said, leading Caro toward a row of plastic chairs.

"I can't answer that," Caro said, though she wasn't exactly sure Max had made the comment to get a reply. It almost seemed as if he was talking to himself, trying to sort through everything.

"We weren't planning to get married," he said, lowering himself to a seat with Bethany. "But we were friends. We were good to each other."

This was the conversation that had gotten them in trouble two nights ago, but this time Caro decided to talk to him as if she didn't know his history, as if he was any other confused single dad she was hired to help because, really, that's what he was. He wasn't trying to convince her of anything. He was trying to sort out the situation for himself.

She faced him. "Did you and Linda ever actually talk about what you would do if she got pregnant?''

His expression clouded. ''No.''

''Okay, then she probably believed that you had no interest and she made the choices she thought best.''

Caro hadn't intended to draw a comparison to the past or make him feel guilty, but that comment could as easily be applied to Mary Catherine Connor as to Linda Russell. The second it was out of her mouth she regretted it.

But Max didn't react. As if the situation with Mary Catherine hadn't happened, he said, ''Linda and I knew each other better than that. And,'' he added pointedly, as if he had just remembered this tidbit, ''she was on the Pill. We never talked about a possible pregnancy because we didn't think there would be one.''

Caro looked at him. ''She was on the Pill?''

''That's what she told me.''

''Oh my gosh, Max,'' Caro said, a thought striking her that was so obvious and so simple it was staggering. ''What if she got pregnant deliberately? What if she wanted a baby…a beautiful baby…with a smart, talented person, and she used you to get one.''

Max combed his fingers through his hair.

"Was she the kind of woman to go off on her own, so to speak, and do something like that?"

Max squeezed his eyes shut. "I hate to say this, but Linda could do just about anything. She was very independent and strong willed."

"She wanted this baby, but she didn't want you to know because she didn't want you involved. My guess is she didn't want *any* man involved. She simply wanted a baby. You already told me that you both knew you two wouldn't get married, so she probably knew you wouldn't try too hard to contact her once she left you."

"It all makes sense," Max said, shaking his head.

Caro put her hand on his forearm. "Don't think too poorly of her."

Max shook his head again. "I don't. I mean, I don't completely understand, but I've been with the FBI long enough to know we can never really comprehend what motivates someone." He paused, stared at Caro's fingers on his forearm for several seconds, then caught her gaze.

For what felt like an eternity he searched her eyes and Caro knew why. When she touched his arm, a sharp jolt of electricity shot through her. She didn't think he had felt it, but he had. They shared some kind of chemistry. It was why she kept trying to give him the benefit of the doubt, and why he had gotten angry at her two nights before. He cared what she thought about him because he liked her. Gorgeous, interesting, FBI agent Max Riley found simple small-town teacher Caro Evans attractive.

"And in the same way that I know when it's futile to try to figure out somebody's motives, I also know when it's futile to go after something I can't have because of circumstances in my life." With his eyes and those words he quite clearly told her that he might find her attractive and he might also realize she found him attractive, too, but there wasn't a darned thing he could do about it. "I'm sorry I got mad at you the other night. I shouldn't have."

"That's okay," Caro whispered, holding his gaze.

"No, it's not. I made some choices a lot of years ago based on the very youthful belief that I was doing the right thing, the best thing for everyone involved. Turns out I was wrong." He paused again, searching her eyes, obviously gauging her reaction. "And though I know this is probably going to be very hard for you to believe, I can't take back that choice now."

"Would you, if you could?"

"Absolutely."

"Then you need to try."

He shook his head. "You don't understand. I can't."

"You—"

"Can't," Max said, interrupting her. "And I'm also starving. Is it possible for a person to have lunch while holding a baby?"

He had changed the subject and Caro knew why. His mind was made up. Whatever reason he had for not accepting responsibility for Mary Catherine's baby, he couldn't change it. And nothing Caro said or did would sway that belief. She didn't know him well enough to try anyway. And, of course, it was none of her business.

"Sure, it's more than possible to eat lunch while holding a baby," she said, because dropping the subject was the right thing to do. She rose from her plastic airport chair and reached for Bethany so Max could more easily stand. There was no point to their trying to figure out this attraction when they couldn't follow up on it. "And I'm just the person to teach you how, because I'm starving, too."

Chapter Three

Caro walked into the kitchen of her parents' home to find three of her five adult siblings doing dishes.

"Hey! Look who's home. It's the world traveler," dark-haired Sadie said as she returned the salt and pepper shakers to a rack beneath the oak cabinets. Caro's older sister by two years, Sadie had both the dark hair and green eyes of the Evans family. In fact, she took after their father's relatives so much, she was almost identical to his youngest sister, who was also her namesake, the Sadie Evans who owned the day care.

Caro dropped her suitcase on the shiny red-brick-pattern tile floor. "Some world traveler. I barely got out of the hotel."

"Ick. Don't say that!" Hannah, the youngest

of the clan said, pulling a plate from the sudsy water, rinsing it and setting it in the dish drainer. Blond like Caro, but with the family's trademark green eyes, twenty-four-year-old Hannah was a knockout. "You were with Max Riley. Saying you never got out of the hotel room dredges up all kinds of mental pictures we don't want to get."

"Hannah!" Luke said in reprimand. Tall and lean, Caro's sandy-haired brother had been a high-school football star with Max Riley. Both had been on the team that ruled the town for the three years it dominated its division and brought "fame" to the area when it won the state championship. Popular Luke had a dish towel in his hands, but Caro had never actually seen him dry a dish in his life.

"That's disgusting," he continued. "Besides, the Max Riley jokes are getting old. Don't you have somebody else you can pick on? After fourteen years, I think it's time we let the poor guy alone."

"You're only saying that because he's your friend," Sadie said.

"No, I'm saying it because fourteen years is a long time and I think it's time to move on."

"If Maria were here," Sadie said, "I'm sure

she would remind you that it's hard to forget a thirteen-year-old child.''

"Yeah, Luke," Caro said. Though her voice was softer and kinder than Sadie's, she still understood what Sadie was saying. "We can't simply forget about Brett."

Luke huffed out something about being outnumbered, tossed his dish towel to the counter and left the room.

"Damn. He got away without doing the dishes again," Sadie said, grabbing his red-and-white-checked dish towel from the countertop.

"You played right into his hands," Hannah said. "For somebody who is supposed to outsmart criminals for a living," Hannah continued, referring to the fact that Sadie was a detective in Pittsburgh, "you're not very bright when it comes to dealing with Luke."

"Whatever," Sadie said, her blunt-cut black hair swinging as she shook her head in disgust. "I just hate the way he defends Max Riley. That's all."

Caro had bent to pick up her suitcase, but she bit her lower lip and straightened again. "I'm not so sure he's wrong."

Sadie gasped noisily. "Caro!"

"I know we can't completely forget the past. But we can't go on unconditionally hating Max, either," Caro said, leaning against the counter as she watched Hannah wash dishes and Sadie dry them. "You should have seen him with his daughter. He's determined to be a good father."

"Did you ever stop to think that that little girl got a nice big fat check from the government when her mommy was killed in the line of duty?"

"And you think Max took her for the money?" Caro asked incredulously.

"Oh, please. You are such a babe in the woods," Sadie said, rolling her eyes as she dried a cup. "People like Max Riley never do anything without a reason."

"I suppose," Caro said, thinking that did make a weird kind of sense, especially since he'd spent money like water the days they were in Las Vegas. "But it's just that he was so sweet with that baby."

Sadie gave Caro a raised-eyebrow look. "Impressing you, maybe?"

"I doubt it," Caro said, though she felt her cheeks redden guiltily.

Because of her curse of being pale, her sisters noticed. Sadie clucked her tongue. "He did. He made a pass at you, didn't he?"

"No," Caro said, because he hadn't. He wanted to. She knew that. But he wouldn't. He said he couldn't. "He did not make a pass at me.

But while we were away I did get the distinct impression that he's grown up since high school, which I'd like to say you also did, Sadie. So why is it possible for you to be different, but not Max Riley?''

''Because I don't have a thirteen-year-old son being raised by a single mother.''

''Maybe he regrets that?''

''Then why doesn't he go meet Brett? Why doesn't he pay child support?'' Sadie sighed. ''He might have grown up, but he grew up on his terms. And he's not taking responsibility for Brett. Until he does, he's not much of a man in my eyes.''

Sadie threw down her dish towel as if the whole conversation disgusted her, and she stormed out of the room.

''Now it's just me doing the dishes,'' Hannah said.

''Sorry about that,'' Caro said. She picked up the towel. ''I'll help.''

''No. You go unpack. I'm fine,'' Hannah said with a slight smile. ''I was teasing. Trying to lighten the mood.''

''I appreciate that.''

''Your mood's not going to lighten, though, is it?''

Caro looked at her little sister. "I don't think so."

"He was *that* nice?"

"Not just nice," Caro said, fumbling for an explanation. "He was…sincere. It was hard for me to reconcile that he would desert a child. Yet, he said he had good reasons for things he did in the past and couldn't change his decisions now."

Hannah gasped. "He talked about it?"

Caro shook her head. "Only in vague terms."

"Well, I hate to say this, Caro, but I'm with Sadie on this. The man has a son being raised by a single mother who barely makes ends meet. And he doesn't even acknowledge him. That's not right."

"No," Caro agreed, reaching for her suitcase. "It isn't."

She walked out of the kitchen and down the hall, on her way to her second-floor bedroom. When she reached the foyer stairway, she saw her parents sitting in the living room and set her suitcase beside the step.

"I'm home."

"Hey, Caro!" Her father, Peter Evans, enthusiastically leaped from his chair and ran to the entryway to give Caro a hug. A tall man with dark hair and green eyes, he didn't look a day over forty, yet he was edging toward sixty. "Welcome home."

Caro's mother set her crocheting on her lap as Caro walked into the room. Just as Sadie had all the Evans family features, Caro had her mother's blond hair and brown eyes. "How did the trip go?"

"It was long." She blew her breath out on a sigh as she sat on the rocker across from her mother. "And confusing."

Her father instantly became alert. "You didn't have any trouble, did you?"

She shook her head.

"I didn't think she would," Lily Evans said confidently, picking up her crocheting as if to close that part of the discussion. Not to defend Max Riley, but as a show of support for Caro's competence as an adult. "But we're glad you're finally home because Sadie Senior had a little trouble today."

Concerned for her dad's youngest sister who had been under the weather lately, Caro asked, "What kind of trouble?"

"She's still feeling awful," Caro's dad said. "Tired mostly."

"We sent her to see a doctor in Pittsburgh and he admitted her to the hospital for tests," Lily added, catching Caro's gaze. "This afternoon we divided up her workload, but since you always work in the single-dad school in the summer, we decided you could just take over completely.''

"That's not a problem," Caro said immediately. "It's summer vacation. I can run it for the next couple of months."

"Good, because until somebody figures out what's wrong with her," Pete said, "I'm not letting Sadie go back to work. It's not right for a forty-eight-year-old woman to be exhausted all the time."

"I can help at the day care, too," Caro said, but her father interrupted her.

"Your mother and I will manage the day care. You just take care of the single-dad school."

"Okay," Caro said, rising from the rocker. "I'm going to unpack."

Caro was in her bedroom only a few minutes later when her cell phone rang. She popped it open. "Hello."

"Hello? Sadie Evans?"

Realizing her parents must have already call forwarded the emergency line for the single-dad school to her cell phone, Caro said, "This is Caro Evans. I'm taking over the single-dad school for my aunt this week. How can I help you?"

"Oh, hi, Caro. This is Max Riley."

Because Bethany was crying in the background, Max was yelling. Even so, Caro could barely hear him. "Look, I'm sorry to bother you, but—"

"Stop, Max," she said, shouting into the phone, knowing her voice was also competing with Bethany's loud sobbing. "I can hardly hear you. It's easier for me if you just answer a few quick questions. Are you holding Bethany?"

"Yes."

Caro shoved a finger in her ear and pressed the phone to the other. "Because you can't get her to stop crying?"

"Yes."

"And you need me to come over?"

"Yes."

"All right. Hold on. I'll be there in a few minutes."

She snapped the phone closed, grabbed her purse and ran out of her bedroom. At the bottom of the steps she called into the living room, "Remember how you told me the single-dad school was my responsibility?"

"Yes," her dad said, walking out of the living room, into the foyer where Caro stood beside the stained-glass front door.

"Well, I just got my first emergency call." She kissed her dad's cheek. "Wish me luck."

"Okay. Luck," he said, laughing as he opened the door for her.

Caro ran outside, toward the garage, but remembering Max's grandfather's house was only a few blocks away, she decided it would be silly to take her car. However, with Bethany's crying still ringing in her ears, her brisk walk became a modified run. By the time she jogged up the back steps of the quaint redbrick and stone Cape Cod house that had belonged to Max's grandparents, she was out of breath.

Max turned on the porch light and opened the door, Bethany over his shoulder, sobbing.

"Oh, my goodness," Caro said, sympathy for the baby immediately overriding any greeting. "Come here," she said, taking Bethany from Max. She cuddled Bethany to her and began to pat her back. The baby immediately wiped her nose on Caro's shoulder. "Wow, her face is wet," Caro said, following Max through the mudroom and into the kitchen. Sunny yellow curtains, canisters and decorations complemented the pale knotty-pine cabinets and table and chairs.

"Well, her diaper isn't. I changed it four times hoping that was her problem." He blew his breath out on a tired sigh. "It wasn't."

Caro sat on one of the chairs, putting Bethany on her lap. "Did you feed her?"

"I followed your instructions, which were almost word for word what the Russells had written on a sheet I found in one of the diaper bags."

"Okay," Caro said, studying the little girl's red-rimmed eyes. As if understanding she was in the hands of a professional, Bethany began to calm down. Her sobbing became hiccuppy sounds. Caro opened the baby's mouth and felt along her gums. "Hmm. I'm guessing part of the problem is that she's teething. But, realistically, we both know the other part of the problem is that she misses her grandparents and familiar surroundings."

She glanced up and saw Max leaning against the kitchen counter, looking exhausted and staring at her as if she held the answers to the secrets of the universe. The way he gazed at her sent a shiver of awareness through her, but she ignored it. Right now he would gaze adoringly at any woman who could help him with Bethany.

"And there's a three-hour time difference between here and Vegas that's probably throwing her off balance, too."

"Great," Max said, combing his fingers through his thick black hair. "It seems like everything is stacked against me. Not only is poor Bethany frightened, confused, teething and tired, but I'm not the best choice of a person to help her through all this."

Caro laughed. "Hey, come on. Some of the most unlikely people become very good parents. If they can do it, you can do it."

"Right."

"I mean it. You, at least, are interested. You should see some of the guys at the single-dad school."

As Caro spoke, exhausted Bethany snuggled against her breasts, getting comfortable. The lids of the baby's eyes were swollen from crying, making them heavy enough that even Bethany's stubbornness couldn't keep them raised, and they drifted closed. Caro knew the child would be asleep any second, and she angled her chin toward the baby so Max would notice. He nodded and smiled, then returned his gaze to Caro's.

"Anyway," Caro said, modulating her voice to a soothing, even tone. "Because you're actually interested, you'll catch on to all of this a lot quicker."

He took a deep breath. "I hope so. I hate to see her suffer like this."

"I know," Caro said, recognizing his genuine concern for Bethany. "But I'm not going to lie to you, Max. Raising a baby's not easy. It's damn hard under normal circumstances. You have a little girl who lost her mother and was just taken from the only family she knows. You've got your work cut out for you.''

He nodded in the direction of the baby. "She's sleeping."

"Do you have a crib set up?"

"That's the one of the things I did manage to get done before I left for Vegas."

"Well, that was good thinking."

"Should I take her?" Max asked as Caro started to rise.

She shook her head. "It's going to be risky enough when we lay her down in her crib. Let's save our jostling for that one major event."

Caro followed Max up the stairs to a small room at the right of a little cubbyhole that served as a meeting place for all the doors of the upstairs rooms. "This is cute."

Max smiled. "I've always loved this house. It has personality."

"It has window seats," Caro said with a quiet gasp of pleasure as Max led her into the nearly empty room on the right. A new crib sat in the center on top of pale-blue carpeting. Nursery characters decorated the yellow, blue and pink print wallpaper and the pillow of the window seat. But the paper was old and dusty, as were the white lace curtains on the window. "Your grand-parents had a nursery?"

Max nodded. "For visitors. My aunt's family lived in Ohio. When they stayed here, the kids used this room. After everybody outgrew cribs, they bought beds. Those wore out, and about two years ago we tossed them. But my grandparents kept the wallpaper." He smiled at the memory. "They liked it."

"Well, it's cute," Caro whispered, sliding the baby into her crib. "But it could probably use some cleaning."

Max glanced around as if considering the idea. "That makes sense. Not only would that be better for Bethany, but it might also enhance the resale value of the house." He jutted his chin in the direction of the sleeping baby. "What now?"

"Now I think we better go downstairs and let her sleep. Do you have a baby monitor?"

"That was also in one of the diaper bags. I set it up in the kitchen."

"Then we can go."

"We don't need to cover her or anything?"

"Max, it's June."

"Okay," he said, but lagged behind, and Caro tilted her head in question.

"I feel like I should kiss her good-night or something."

"Oh, I'm sorry!" Caro said. "You can kiss her good-night. Just be very careful about it. We don't want her to awaken."

He nodded and Caro decided to leave the room. She walked out of the bedroom and was in the kitchen checking the baby monitor when Max came downstairs.

"Now what?" he asked as he stepped into the spotlessly clean room. Given the less-than-perfect state of the rest of the house, Caro recognized making this room livable had probably been the first job he tackled when he arrived in Wilburn.

"Now, we need to talk about a couple of things. First, you obviously signed up for single-dad school. Otherwise, you wouldn't have had the emergency number."

"I'm here for another few weeks. Your Aunt Sadie told me it would be a good idea."

"It is. In fact, you should get yourself to a single-dad class tomorrow."

Max frowned. "There are actual classes?"

"Yes. I haven't seen the schedule yet, so I don't know what age groups are taking lessons, but there's always a class at ten o'clock. I'll be the teacher. If you come by a little after nine tomorrow we can do the paperwork."

"What else?"

"I think I should stay a few more hours tonight, in case she wakes up. You're charged a flat fee for the visit, so it doesn't matter if I leave immediately or at two o'clock in the morning, and this way we can use the time to answer practical questions you might have, now that you've spent a few hours alone with Bethany.''

"Okay, but I haven't eaten and I'm starving. You don't mind if I have a sandwich while we talk?"

Caro grimaced. "Actually, I'm starving, too. I got home too late for dinner, got caught up in unpacking and I forgot to eat."

"Good," Max said, his mood lightening. "I'm usually forced to eat alone, but I hate to. I'd rather have company."

"Me, too."

"Are bacon, lettuce and tomato sandwiches all right with you?" he asked, opening the refrigerator to begin rummaging for the things he needed.

"They sound great," Caro said. "Can I help with anything?"

"No, you sit at the table and talk while I microwave the bacon." He paused, and peered around the refrigerator door to look at Caro. "I need every minute of instruction I can get about this job."

"The toughest job you'll ever love."

"I hope so. Because you realize if I screw up, I screw up the life of another person."

"You'll be fine."

"Like I said, I hope so." He opened the bacon package. "Start at the beginning."

"I'm not sure what you would call the beginning, but we'll start with what you're going to do tomorrow when she wakes up."

"Right."

"She's going to wake up wet," Caro said frankly. "But she'll also be hungry. You have to decide if it's more important to wash her or feed her."

"How will I know?"

"Oh, you'll know," Caro said, then she laughed.

Max stopped, thought about that, and grimaced. "Point taken."

"Usually, it's best to create a routine," she continued. "For instance, if she gets accustomed to getting bathed and dressed before she goes downstairs to eat, she won't rebel about having to wait for breakfast on those days when she *has to* be bathed before she can go downstairs."

"Okay, so if I start that routine tomorrow, eventually she'll get used to it."

"Right. But you have to remember that feeding

can also be sloppy, so you need to use bibs or you'll be bathing her again.''

"This is complicated.''

"Not really. In a few days you'll be a pro.''

"Right,'' he said as he arranged bacon on a microwave plate. "Keep going.''

"She needs stimulation. She might take a quick nap after she eats, but when she awakens she needs you to play with her, talk to her, read to her, or something.''

Max stared at her incredulously. "How do mothers get any work done?''

Caro laughed. "Mothers usually set their babies in high chairs...which I note you don't have yet...while they do their work.''

"I'll go to the mall as soon as I can.''

"As they wash the dishes, iron clothes, scrub the floor and cook dinner, mothers maintain a running stream of chatter with their baby. Or they tell stories, like fairy tales that everybody knows, so they don't have to hold a book and their hands are free to do other things.''

"That makes sense, but how do I handle that when I get back home and have to leave her to go to work?''

"If it were me, I would cuddle her for a few minutes right before I left and for a few minutes immediately after I arrived home. Then I would put her in the high chair so I could chat with her while I fixed myself supper. Nine chances out of ten, your nanny will have already fed Bethany by that time.''

Leaning against the counter as the bacon cooked, he nodded, and Caro felt the strange mix of emotions she had been feeling all along about this man. He was too interested, too good with Bethany, too sweet and considerate to be the cruel villain her sisters claimed he was. And just like always, when her defenses dropped, attraction warmed her blood. Not just because he was gorgeous, but because he was genuinely nice.

She cleared her throat and said, ''But even though she will have already eaten, Bethany can still be your company while you eat.''

''That's a perk.''

''See, there are benefits already to having this baby.''

''Really.''

They continued to talk about Bethany as Max fixed the sandwiches, but as they ate, Max ran out of questions and Caro couldn't think of anything else to say. The conversation easily slipped into a discussion of her qualifications to take over the single-dad school, and before she knew it, Caro was telling Max the story of her life—specifically, the story of her last real boyfriend.

"He dumped you?"

"Unceremoniously. After college, I easily got my job here, but he had a little trouble deciding where he wanted to work, so he moved back in with his parents in Pittsburgh. We talked on the phone, visited a few weekends, then he got a job but never told me where, and one day I realized he had stopped calling."

"If it took you a few weeks to realize he'd stopped calling, you must not have missed him much."

"I was very excited about my first job."

"Which doesn't say a whole hell of a lot about him as a boyfriend."

Caro laughed. "I suppose."

"And that was it? That was your one great romance?"

"Unless you want to count my high-school sweetheart."

"Who was?"

"Joshua Neibert."

"I don't remember him."

"You were long gone," Caro said, to explain why Max didn't recognize the name.

"Yeah, that's probably it." He paused, considered, then said, "Did he play football?"

"No."

"*That's* why I don't remember him."

"Don't tell me you kept up with the team!"

Max laughed. "Hey, the team I was on had a record. Periodically, I check in to make sure it's still standing."

"While you were at college they all but built a shrine to you, Luke, Jake Malloy and Rory Brennan."

Max stiffened slightly. Not a lot, but enough so that Caro noticed, and she stopped speaking. He didn't mind talking about his team. Yet, somehow, that last comment had taken a step into forbidden territory. She could see that from the hardened expression on Max's face. The only guess she had for why her words offended him was that leaving for college reminded him of Mary Catherine...or of Mary Catherine getting pregnant.

He rose from his seat, gathered the dishes and took them to the sink. "I was supposed to go out with Luke this weekend, but I guess that's off since I can't take a baby to Turner's Tavern."

"The day care has a list of qualified babysitters. The night out doesn't have to be off, as long as you don't plan on drinking yourself silly."

"I outgrew my need to get drunk years and years and years ago," Max said with a chuckle. "And what do you mean when you say qualified?"

"Sadie Senior doesn't recommend someone unless he or she has completed the training provided at the hospital in Johnstown. Though most of the people on the list are teenagers, they have had several weeks of training. By the time they are certified, they know what they're doing. Plus, we recommend our single dads leave the single dad emergency number with the sitter."

"This single-dad school is starting to sound like a bargain."

"I keep telling Sadie Senior she needs to charge more."

Max burst out laughing at the very second that a burst of crying erupted from the monitor.

Caro grinned. "Duty calls."

"Right."

Max led Caro up the steps, and she watched as he checked Bethany's diaper and discovered it was wet. She almost volunteered to do the job, if only because he could be tired of it by now, but he didn't pause long enough for her to say anything. He just began to change the diaper, and Caro realized it hadn't even entered his mind to turn to her for help the way most of the men she and Sadie trained usually did. Taking care of the baby had become second nature to him. In less than twenty-four hours he saw himself as Bethany's primary caregiver.

Again, the odd, confusing feeling engulfed her. But she told herself to ignore it. What happened in Max Riley's past wasn't her business. Particularly since it was now her responsibility to train him for his future. She couldn't let anything about him or his life affect her ability to teach him.

Max rocked the baby to sleep while Caro sat on the window seat nodding her approval every time he did something soothing and comforting like stroke Bethany's hair or whisper endearments.

"The important thing," she told him as they walked down the stairs, "is that she feels secure. The more she understands that you love her, the better she will feel. The better she feels, the better she will behave."

"So I need to tell her I love her a lot?"

"More than that. You need to use a soothing tone of voice, keep her comfortable, fed and dry, and pay oodles of attention to her."

"Got it," Max said, collapsing on the sofa. "I suppose you'll be leaving now?"

Caro shook her head. "No. If she woke up once, she could wake up again. Because this is your first night together as dad and daughter, I think it's a good idea for me to wait around for at least one more wake-up call."

"You won't worry about what people will say

you were doing in here with me when they see you leaving my house in the middle of the night?''

It was the first time they'd hit both the attraction and his reputation head-on, and initially Caro was stunned into silence. He was so darned good-looking that a picture of them making out on his sofa all night instantly popped into her head—the same way it would be popping into the mind of every other resident who saw her leave. Though that idea should have sobered her, all the thought of necking with him seemed to do was make her want to shiver in anticipation.

''I'm here for a single-dad appointment,'' she said, not really wanting to draw a line in their relationship, but doing so anyway because neither one of them was ready for the image that jumped into her brain. In spite of the way just looking at him made her pulse simmer, he had a reputation and so did she. Though he might not mind enhancing his, as a teacher she needed to keep hers just the way it was. Pristine.

She glanced around, looking for a way to pass the time innocently. ''Let's watch television.''

''Okay,'' Max agreed. He tossed the channel guidebook to Caro. ''You pick the program. I'll hunt for the remote control.''

When he found the remote, he handed it to Caro, who sat on the recliner and set the station.

Max lay down on the sofa. After a few minutes, Caro found a detective show that looked like a winner, and she pushed her chair into the reclining position to relax and enjoy the program. As she did, she noticed Max was already asleep. Knowing she would be entertained by the television program, Caro decided to let him alone, particularly since this might be the only rest he got all night. But because he was asleep, that put her completely in charge of Bethany. Not trusting her hearing, she retrieved the baby monitor from the kitchen and put it on the end table beside her chair.

Ready to watch the show, Caro fixed her gaze on the television screen, but every couple of minutes her eyelids drooped. She fought sleep until she was so drowsy, she couldn't remember why she was doing it, and eventually she let herself drift off, too.

The chirping of birds awakened her several hours later and she bounced up on the recliner with a start.

All her muscles ached in protest from having slept on a chair, but she didn't groan until she noticed that the VCR clock said 6:05. Not only would her parents be worried, but also it was too early to get up and too late to go back to bed once she got home. But when her gaze strayed to Max, still sleeping soundly on the sofa, she stifled a giggle.

Not only had he slept in blue jeans, he also still wore his tennis shoes. Realizing he must have been exhausted to sleep through the night in jeans and tennis shoes, she decided not to disturb him but to let him get all the rest he could before Bethany woke.

Caro stretched the kinks out of her back and muscles before she rose from the chair, and the entire time she watched Max. Not because he was handsome—though he was, incredibly so, especially with the dark stubble that had grown on his chin and cheeks—but because he was a puzzle.

With him sound asleep and the world a murky, silent place, she walked closer to the sofa and looked down at him.

He was an FBI agent. A tough guy, if the rumors about his job and the way he performed his job were true. Yet, he was soft and sweet with his baby girl. He supposedly had a son he ignored. Yet, he hadn't argued beyond asking for a DNA test when the Russells asked him to come for Bethany.

He and his life just didn't make any sense.

She inched a little nearer, studying his face,

seeing that the worry lines from the day before had been eased by sleep, examining a shock of hair that fell to his forehead and noticing the way his dark eyebrows arched.

He really was adorable, she thought, smiling as she knelt beside the sofa. Physically handsome and very nice, he was the epitome of everything a wise woman looked for in a man.

She gave in to the irresistible urge to comb her fingers through his soft black hair. She didn't know what she felt for him, but she did know she neither mistrusted him nor hated him. He was a good person, a hardworking, honest man who would use every resource at his disposal to care for his daughter. The only side of Max Riley she knew was the good side. In fact, if she were to judge him based only on what she saw, how he behaved, how he reacted, how he treated her and Bethany, Caro would have to say she liked him.

She liked him. The conclusion floated into her brain as softly as a baby angel.

She liked him.

What an odd situation, she thought as she allowed her finger to trace the shape of his face. She liked the most mistrusted, disliked person in town because he had never given her reason to mistrust or dislike him. He had been nothing but good to her.

Caro licked her suddenly dry lips and found herself staring at Max's mouth, and she had to admit she didn't merely like him in a platonic way. She was attracted to him in the way a woman was attracted to a man she was considering for a husband or lover, and she wondered what it would be like to kiss him. She had heard the stories, of course. But in the same way she couldn't mistrust him based on rumors, she couldn't believe the stories about his masterful lovemaking until she experienced it.

The thought almost made her giggle. Her sisters would die before they let her go out with him. She would never make love with him, probably never kiss him.

She lightly traced the shape of his mouth.

It seemed a pity.

In fact, it seemed such a shame, that she bent and brushed her lips across his lightly. She glimpsed the soft texture of his mouth, the slightly salty taste, but that hardly satisfied her curiosity or mitigated the sense of injustice that brewed inside her realizing she would never kiss him, never really know him, because of things that happened fourteen years ago. Things that didn't add up. Things that seemed so far removed from the man he was now that she couldn't associate them with the man he was today. All she knew was that this

man, this Max Riley on the sofa, didn't deserve
to be hated.

On that firm conclusion, she rose and left the
living room. In the kitchen she found paper and
wrote a note explaining that Bethany must have
slept through the night, because she and Max had,
and she had gone home a little after six. She reminded him to come to the day care for single-
dad class, then walked outside into the muggy
June morning.

Lost in thought, she ran down the driveway to
the sidewalk and ducked just in time when a
newspaper flew by her ear.

"Hey, sorry, Caro."

"Brett!" Caro said as he screeched his bike to
a stop beside her. Halfway between a boy and a
man, Brett was well over five feet, and if he grew
into his overlong arms and legs, he would probably be the size of a basketball player. His blond-
brown hair fell across his forehead and he swiped
it away to reveal his pretty blue eyes.

He grimaced. "I didn't see you."

"I didn't see you, either," Caro said, smiling
at him, noting how handsome he was becoming
and that he would undoubtedly be a heartbreaker
when he reached his twenties.

"Are you taking your morning walk?"

Caro shook her head. "No. I had a single-dad appointment last night."

"Oh," Brett said, glancing behind her at Max's granddad's house. He bit his lip, then said, "I guess I better go."

"Yeah," Caro said, fighting a grimace at her own stupidity for not choosing her words more carefully. She had no idea how much Brett knew or how much he guessed, but she could see he knew something. Probably that Max was his dad and Max was here in Wilburn.

Brett rode away, tossing newspapers on porches as he maneuvered his bike down the street, and Caro stared after him. She liked him. She liked Mary Catherine. But she also liked Max.

She liked Max.

And she knew she had better get accustomed to that thought, because if it was difficult for her to acknowledge, it was going to be a hundred times more difficult for her sisters to accept. Sadie would yell and Maria would pout.

But fair was fair.

She liked Max Riley...and not just as a friend.

Chapter Four

As Max approached the day-care center for his first single-dad class, he didn't know what to expect. He accepted that most of the people in Wilburn disliked him, so he didn't anticipate a warm reception. In the week before going to Las Vegas to pick up Bethany, he had ducked more than his fair share of slings and arrows and thinly veiled accusations in the grocery store and at the gas station, but he'd refused to let it bother him. And he wouldn't let it bother him today if somebody said something.

Seeing Caro Evans again was what had his stomach tied in knots. He had not dreamed that she had kissed him before she left his house that morning. He had felt her lips touch his because he had been wide awake, not really feigning sleep by keeping his eyes closed, but not about to interrupt whatever thought process had brought her to his side.

Breathless and tingling with anticipation, he hadn't dared stop or confuse her, because he needed to know what she felt. Every time he looked at her his heart leaped to his throat and he had a sense that he wasn't supposed to meet her and walk away never to see her again. She was a beautiful, wonderful woman, and he liked her so much it was the first time he reconsidered the choices he'd made about Mary Catherine Connor, because the ramifications of those decisions precluded everyone in Wilburn, including Caro, from liking him.

But she did like him. She had kissed him. And though he had no clue what they were supposed to do now, he did know he wasn't letting the opportunity slip away.

The day care was in the back of Sadie Evans's two-story beige frame house. As Max strode down the sidewalk to the entryway, he saw Caro's parents in the fenced-in backyard, leading twenty or so children in two different games. The older kids played kickball on one side of the yard with Caro's dad. The younger ones were in the opposite corner, enjoying a rousing game of Wiffleball with her mother. He didn't disturb the couple by calling out hello. For starters, they might not hear him, but the truth was, he wasn't yet ready to see if they would acknowledge him. At one time they had been like second parents to him, and if they treated him coolly, that would hurt almost as much as it would hurt if Caro pretended this morning there wasn't something going on between them.

He jogged up the three steps to the porch, opened the screen door and walked into a small space that looked to be a coatroom with waist-high hooks, and shelves that were probably for hats and mittens. Caro stood with her back to him, pulling magazines out of the mail that had just been delivered.

"Hi."

She turned and faced him with her bright smile. "Hi." After setting the mail on a shoulder-high shelf, undoubtedly designed to keep things like the mail out of the hands of children, she reached for Bethany and pulled her from his arms. "And hello to you too, sweetie," she said, tickling Bethany's tummy. "How are you today?"

"She eats like a horse," Max said, and Bethany started to laugh, but it was an odd snorting sound that mixed too much breathing with laughter. "And she sounds like a donkey."

Caro clicked her tongue. "Oh, your daddy is

bad,'' she said, scolding Max more with the look she gave him than with what she said, but Bethany only laughed harder. Caro shook her head. ''Trust me, Bethany, in a few years you won't think that's funny.''

''So, where's the school?'' Max asked, glancing beyond the coatroom.

''There really is no school, per se,'' Caro said, directing Max to a big open space. Two cribs, two play yards, a bassinet and a changing table lined the far wall. Bookcases and toy bins rimmed the wall on the right. Shelves filled with toys created the left wall. ''Classes are held here in the playroom.''

''And where's everybody else?''

''Not here yet. And there's something else you need to know. Right now, Bethany would be the only baby enrolled. All the other kids are three and older.''

''Wrong end of a baby boom?'' Max asked as Caro grabbed a fuzzy lime-green carpet from a stash atop a bookcase. She set the carpet in one of the play yards and sat Bethany on the carpet.

''You better believe it,'' Caro said. ''That's why Sadie created the single-dad school. There are three day cares in Wilburn and she wasn't getting enough kids to meet expenses, let alone make a decent living. So she started the classes to draw in business, and the concept evolved into what you're getting now.''

"I think it's a fine idea.''

Caro smiled at him and, as always, his heart flip-flopped and his mind went completely blank. Simple, pretty Caro Evans had him reacting like a teenager again.

"You're exactly why Aunt Sadie came up with the single-dad school,'' she said. Having found a few toys for Bethany, she set them in the play yard beside her. "But it still doesn't bring in enough business. In fact, she's going to bid on the Sunbright Solutions day care contract.''

"Sunbright Solutions? Isn't that the company Troy Cramer started?'' Max asked, referring to Wilburn's most distinguished son. Troy had been a computer nerd in high school, so no one was surprised when he started a software company that blossomed into a billion-dollar industry.

"Yep. But he moved home about six months ago, which was also a year after his wife died, and he's been running the company long-distance from his estate outside of town. When he had his preliminary talk with Roy Johnson at the bank, Troy told him he was tired of traveling back and forth so he's moving the company here.''

Max whistled. "That would certainly pick up the local economy.''

"Most of his employees are coming with the company. And that means more kids, so Sadie's applied for a mortgage on the house so she can build on to accommodate the additional children."

"She's a forward thinker."

"Yeah."

A quiver in her voice alerted Max that something was wrong. "What's up?" he asked, trying not to be nosy but unable to stop the immediate flare of panic. He couldn't stand the thought of something hurting Caro, and, whatever this problem, it hurt her.

Caro cleared her throat. "Well, it's just that Sadie Senior is...well, she has been a little sick lately."

"Oh."

"It's not that bad...at least we don't think so..."

"Yes, you do," Max said, putting everything together. "Your entire family must think it's serious, because your parents are running the day care. You're managing the single-dad school. Sadie can't even do the job she apparently loves." He paused and carefully asked, "How sick is she?"

Caro shrugged. "We don't know. She had an appointment with a doctor in Pittsburgh yesterday. He admitted her into the hospital and ordered tests.''

''That's not good.''

''She's only forty-eight. She can't be too sick,'' Caro said, ruining the positive spirit of her comment when her voice quavered again.

Max turned her around and pulled her into his arms. If she hadn't kissed him that morning, he never would have infringed on her privacy this way. But she liked him. He knew that now.

''Age doesn't matter when it comes to being sick. You know that and it scares you.''

He felt Caro nod, but more than that he felt a million wonderful sensations. She was soft and warm, and came to just the right place against him. If he shifted his head slightly he could put his chin on her hair. It seemed as if this was exactly where she was supposed to be. And holding her was as natural as breathing, as natural and right as taking care of Bethany.

''Yeah, it scares me because she's young but also because I've never seen anybody act like this. She's so tired she sometimes can't get off her couch.''

''But your family is strong. You pull together,'' he said, and suddenly remembered just how strong her sisters were and just how much they pulled together by recalling how they had treated

him in the one short week that spanned Mary
Catherine's pregnancy announcement and his
move to Florida with his parents. They would
hang Caro if they knew she let herself be com-
forted by him.

He stepped away, releasing her.

She smiled sheepishly. ''Thanks,'' she said, rising on tiptoe to kiss his cheek. But before she
could fall to her feet again, Max caught her upper
arms.

''You kissed me this morning,'' he said. The
words were more of an accusation than a comment, because this situation confused him and an-
gered him. If she didn't want to like him, if she
wasn't allowed to like him, she shouldn't have
kissed him.

Her eyes narrowed. ''You were supposed to be
asleep.''

''I was. Sort of. I mean, I didn't feel like getting up yet.''

''So you let me kneel there and stare at you?''
she asked incredulously.

Her righteous indignation appealed to him and
made him forget there were other considerations
than just the two of them. It really didn't take a
lot to get her dander up and when she was angry
she was actually funny.

He smiled. ''I liked it.''

Caro combed her fingers through her hair. "I'm so embarrassed."

"Why?" he asked, stepping close again. Instinct kept taking over when he knew common sense and logic should reign. But he couldn't help it. She attracted him. He wanted her. And something continually pushed him forward, into the territory that should be off limits. "Because you like me or because you're afraid somebody's going to find out?"

"Neither of those."

"Then why?"

"Because I'm an idiot," she said, apparently ignoring the fact that she wasn't supposed to like him. No one was.

"Why do you think you're an idiot?"

"Oh, please," she said, marching over to some scattered toys and rearranging them, as if desperate for something to do. "How many women do you know who kneel by somebody and moon over them?"

"None," Max honestly replied. "I think that's why I liked it." And that *was* why he liked it, he realized. With Caro, there was no artifice. No game playing. That was why she appealed to him. She was who she was and no one told her what to do. *No one.* That was also probably why she wasn't worried about her sisters.

He followed her over to the messy shelf. "So when do *I* get to kiss *you?*"

"Never," she said, but not like a woman avoiding him because of his past. Like a woman who was in the logical stage of confusion that comes in the initial throes of any romance. Particularly since a potential romance between them had more problems than her sisters. He lived in another state. She was six years younger than he was. There were plenty of reasons for her to be wary of a potential relationship between them. Yet, none of those had kept her from kissing him, either.

"I sincerely doubt that," Max said, bending to help her gather the toys. "But I'll let you live with your illusions."

Her face reddened endearingly and Max laughed. "You are so transparent."

She busied herself with the toys again. "As if that doesn't give you an unfair advantage."

He laughed. "Yeah, but so far I haven't used it."

She took a long breath and studied his face for a few seconds. Max felt the weight of her scrutiny, and knew that though her sisters wouldn't stop her if she chose to be with him, they did have all those other problems. Not the least of which was Mary Catherine Connor. From the expression on her face, Caro appeared to be debating if he was worth the trouble.

Finally she smiled. "You're right," she said, shaking her head as if she hadn't made up her mind but hadn't counted him out, either. "So far you haven't used it."

If Caro Evans gave points for honesty, and Max assumed she did, he had just scored big time. But he also sensed he shouldn't push the envelope. Especially not when either one of her parents could walk in on them at any second.

"Okay, then." He glanced around, seeking a way to change the subject. "When do the other guys get here for class?"

She sighed. "Actually, Max, I changed my mind about our course of action for your lessons. Not only is this a toddler session, but also everything worked so well last night that it makes more sense for at least your beginning lessons to be at your house."

It surprised him that she apparently didn't realize what she had suggested, but he wasn't about to let this opportunity pass.

"Good," He walked over and scooped Bethany from the play yard before Caro recognized what she'd said. "Come by at six and I'll have dinner ready."

She stared at him. "You want a lesson tonight?"

"Hey, I'm a desperate man." In three short strides he stood in front of her. "I only have a few weeks here," he said, his voice softening, telling her something she already knew but which he felt worth repeating. "Then Bethany and I go back to Maryland."

He watched her digest that piece of information and wasn't sure if she was processing it from the professional standpoint or a personal one until her gaze casually dropped from his eyes to his mouth.

"You know, I could kiss you right now," he said, if only to see her blush. "I could bend down, kiss you quickly and be gone before you had a chance to yell at me." He saw her eyes cloud at the thought of that and considered it a positive sign that she responded in a sexual way rather than with surprise or indignation. "But you know what? I'm not going to. I owe you a kiss, but I want it to be soft and warm. Romantic," he said, and watched her eyes cloud another notch. That was when his own blood began to heat and his reactions went from tentative to quite clear about what he would like to do.

Before he returned Bethany to the play yard

and did something inappropriate, he turned and strode toward the back door. "I'll see you tonight."

When Caro arrived at Max's grandfather's house at six, she caught the aroma of sizzling steaks. Rather than go to the front door, she followed the scent around the side of the house to the backyard. Sure enough, Max stood by a grill holding a spatula. Bethany sat in a baby swing positioned under the shade of a tree beside a red-wood picnic table. Though she teethed on a thick ring, she pulled it out of her mouth when she saw Caro and began beating it against the swing tray as she made a screeching noise.

"You are a very loud baby," she said, walking over to Bethany who only got louder.

"She likes you," Max said from the stone patio a few feet away from the swing. He waited a heartbeat then added, "Look at my apron."

Caro glanced over at him and saw his neck-to-knees covering that said Kiss the Cook.

"Very funny."

"I am going to kiss you, you know."

"I know," she said, then she sighed. "I suppose I set myself up for that."

"In more ways than you would believe." He turned off the gas for the grill. "She can stay in the swing," Max said, pointing to the picnic table that he had already set and which held store-bought containers of potato salad and baked beans. "We're close enough to entertain her while we eat."

"You're getting very good at this."

"Desperation will make a fast learner out of anybody."

She expected him to take advantage of the privacy of his grandfather's fenced-in backyard to kiss her when he came over to the picnic table, and her entire body began to hum with anticipation. As predicted, he stopped directly in front of her. His eyes smoldered with sexuality, and he stood as close as he could without actually touching her, but he didn't make a move to kiss her. Time stretched out, and with their gazes locked, every second that ticked off the clock made her muscles more taut, her insides more jumpy.

Until she realized he was teasing her. Because she had kissed him, he knew she found him attractive, but that stolen kiss also put him in the position of controlling the game. And he seemed to enjoy having the upper hand. There was a confidence about him that spoke volumes. Though she suspected that as an FBI agent he was probably normally confident, she also knew he hadn't let having a baby throw him for a loop. He had adjusted, but more than that, he had gone out of his way to learn how to be a good father, and that was really why Caro had decided to keep this appointment tonight.

With the afternoon to think through their situation, Caro knew there was no help for the fact that they were attracted to each other. But she also realized something else. Something more obvious. He was a good dad, a *wonderful* dad. Whatever his reason for not acknowledging Brett, be it fear or immaturity, it wasn't valid anymore. And Caro fully intended to make him see that the success he was having with Bethany proved it was time to get involved with his first child. If she was successful, there would be no more reason she and Max Riley couldn't have a relationship.

And then he could kiss her anytime he wanted....

Just the thought almost made her shiver and she stepped back, unable to handle the pressure anymore. ''The steaks look great.''

He appeared to be debating whether or not to let her slip away with such a simple tactic, but soon his confident smile returned and Caro's heart skipped a beat when she realized there was another reason that he hadn't kissed her. He had said he wanted their first kiss to be warm, romantic. He hadn't let her slide away because she was crafty and he wouldn't yank her back because he was stronger. He would wait. And so would she. For the moment he deemed to be perfectly romantic.

He motioned with his hand for her to take a seat at the picnic table. Tingling with anticipation, she sat, and he settled himself on the bench across from her.

Dropping one of the two steaks on a blue plastic plate on the place mat in front of her, he said, "I'm actually a very good cook."

Determined to get her mind off the fact that this man would kiss her, Caro took a bite of her steak and groaned with pleasure. "That's not a wise thing to admit to a working woman."

"I thought it might be a point in my favor."

"It is," she admitted, not about to be coy. If her plan of getting him involved in Brett's life had a hope in hell, she had to be a hundred percent honest with him. Though she wasn't going to allow him to rush her into something for which she wasn't ready, she wouldn't pretend not to be interested when she was. "But you have so many other points, that we're about to step into the land of overkill."

He laughed heartily and they ate dinner sharing comfortable conversation about his job and the class of fifth-graders she'd taught the year before.

Then they washed the dishes together, with Bethany sitting in her safety seat watching them.

"You still didn't get a high chair."

"I'm working up to a trip to the mall. The infant seat is good. She's comfortable and happy there. Not to mention safe."

"No more tantrums?"

He shook his head. "With the exception of the episode our first night together, she's been amazingly good."

"That's because she isn't old enough to make strange yet."

"Make strange?"

"Babies are fairly predictable creatures. They love their parents, but they also aren't picky. They will pretty much behave for anyone who feeds them, keeps them dry or plays with them."

"And here I thought she liked me."

"I'm sure she does. When she's a year old, you probably won't be able to take a shower without her wanting to be in the bathroom with you, but right now she's not too choosy. She would probably go with anybody and adjust to being with them relatively quickly."

Max gaped at her. "Caro, that actually sounds dangerous."

"In a way, it is. That's why parents have to be ultracareful. But in your case right now, you shouldn't argue with Mother Nature. Particularly not when she's working in your favor.''

"Hum-hum," Max said. He dried his hands with a sunny yellow dish towel and then reached for Bethany. "You want to watch me bathe her to make sure I do it right?"

"Okay," Caro said, putting the last piece of silverware in a drawer.

"After her bath, I dress her in pajamas and feed her a bottle and she's in bed by eight."

Caro nodded. "That sounds good."

They walked through the kitchen and hall and then up the steps, with Max holding Bethany and Caro following behind. When they reached the nursery/playroom, Caro could tell from the scent of pine and detergent that it had been cleaned. Even the walls looked scrubbed. "I see you took my suggestion about the walls."

Max shot her a skeptical look. "I don't have an enormous vat of knowledge about germs, but I had my suspicions. I decided I would rather be safe than sorry. So I had the walls and the carpet professionally cleaned this morning so it could be done more quickly than if I did it myself."

Impressed, Caro watched Max bathe Bethany and dress her for bed, then she sat on the window seat observing as he fed her a bottle and rocked her to sleep. She slid off the seat as he carefully laid the baby in the crib and kissed her forehead. Then he directed Caro out of the room, but before he turned out the overhead light, he lit the lamp by the door.

In the little hall outside the bedroom doors, Caro whispered, "You're a natural."

He nodded. "I think so." He gestured for her to go down the steps before him. "Are you leaving?"

Now that Caro had given herself permission to like him, her feelings for him were growing in leaps and bounds, and the truth was, she didn't want to leave. She liked it here. She just plain enjoyed his company.

"I thought maybe I would stay in case she awakens with a problem you can't handle."

"Okay," Max said easily, apparently not recognizing her logic was paper thin.

Caro just barely stopped a sigh of relief. For as much as she didn't want him to think she was running from him, she also didn't want to give him the impression she was throwing herself at him, either.

It was very hard to find the middle ground with a man who was leaving in a few weeks. If he were a permanent resident of Wilburn, a nearby town or even Pittsburgh, Caro could flirt and tease, accept some invitations, decline others, based on her schedule and also a need not to look desperately smitten with someone she had only really known a few days. But with his plan to be out of Wilburn in a couple of weeks, all the rules and games weren't valid.

So, when they went into the living room and Max took a seat on the sofa, Caro continued with her noncoy policy and sat beside him.

"Anything in particular you care to watch on TV?"

"No," she said, smiling slightly. "With six kids in the family, and everybody having different tastes, I grew up learning to like almost every kind of show."

"Are you sure you want to admit that?"

She laughed. "Everybody watches TV. Only unmitigated snobs don't admit it."

That made Max chuckle. "Exactly," he said, and picked up the remote. In line with her instructions, he didn't consult her before he chose a channel. He simply put on a movie.

"How do you still have cable?" Caro asked, careful not to mention that his grandfather had been dead for six months, but also curious because the house did have electricity, running water and even cable.

"We never turned off any of the utilities. My

parents couldn't handle it emotionally. It was like they had a hard time accepting that he was dead.''

"That's awful.''

Max nodded. "After a few months I saw it would be too difficult for my mother to clear out the house, so I volunteered to do it for her. That was when we all realized how long it had been that we had been paying utilities on a house no one lived in and that we couldn't afford the extra expense indefinitely, even though I was waiting around for the call from Linda's attorney. So, I took my leave of absence a few weeks early, left my cell phone number with Linda's lawyer and drove up here.'' He paused and glanced at Caro. "Now I'm glad it all worked out this way. I would have been lost with Bethany by myself in Frederick. Though I know it might not seem like I need a lot of help, it eases my mind to know you're just down the street. I feel as if fate arranged this whole thing, so that I was here for my first few weeks of parenthood, and I could learn the right way to take care of her.''

"You're doing fine,'' Caro said, facing him on the sofa.

He turned, too, and slid one arm along the floral print of the back. "You think so?''

She nodded, suddenly overcome with nerves. Once again, they were alone and they were close.

Except this time they weren't merely close physically, they were also growing close personally. And the mood was different. Romantic, as he had wanted it. If he kissed her, it would be exactly as he told her he wanted it to be.

A few seconds passed with them gazing into each other's eyes, intensifying the intimacy, electrifying the mood. Then, with his one arm already circling her on the sofa, he stretched forward and touched his mouth to hers.

Everything inside Caro melted into warmth. In one kiss it was clear there was more than just a physical attraction between them. They shared the mystical, mythical chemistry everybody had told her about since junior high, but which she herself had never experienced. Something about him seemed to bring out something in her, and though the kiss was tame, though his mouth was warm and soft, Caro knew indescribable passion simmered under the surface. Max held himself in check, but Caro had the distinct impression that what he would like to do was devour her.

But he didn't. He pressed his mouth to hers gently, tentatively, and Caro relaxed enough to kiss him back. Because she wanted to. Not just in response to their physical attraction, not even in response to the chemistry, but because he was one of the most genuinely good men she had ever met.

He was the kind of man that every woman dreamed about, sexy *and* sweet, and right now he was interested in her.

So she kissed him. She opened her mouth when he requested she do so with a nudge from his own, and explosions of delight sprang up inside her. When his arm slid up her back and began to tilt her backward to the sofa, she relaxed enough that momentum and gravity eased her down.

And all the while he kissed her. Sometimes hotly, sometimes sweetly, sometimes hungrily, Max Riley kissed her until Caro felt as if she were drugged. If he had asked her to follow him to the ends of the earth she would have agreed. If he had asked her for anything she would have given it to him. Her money. Her car. Her virtue. The man could have asked her for anything…

And that was when she thought of Mary Catherine Connor. Her sisters had told her that Max was smooth. They had told her that if Mary Catherine could fall for his lines or his kisses, any woman could. And now Caro understood why. Only kissing her, he made her feel things she didn't realize she could feel.

Behind her, Caro heard a dim sound, then a squawk, and she recognized that Bethany was crying at the same time that Max must have heard it. He stopped kissing her, took a second to identify the sound, then glanced at her and whispered, "Bethany."

Caro licked her tingling lips. "You better get her."

"Yeah," he said, and unceremoniously hoisted himself from the couch.

Caro got up, too. Since her reason for staying was to help him with the baby, she also went to Bethany's room. She watched him change her diaper and soothe her back to sleep. And the entire time she thought of Mary Catherine Connor. While Max was off at college, Mary Catherine was a sixteen-year-old mother. Alone. Different. She couldn't even go to the prom her senior year. She hadn't ever had a full-time job, only part-time jobs, so she could care for Brett. She hadn't had a new car, her own apartment or even a vacation separate from her son.

Max finished his duties with Bethany and nodded for Caro to leave the nursery with him. As she walked out, Caro realized Mary Catherine's son hadn't had a nursery. His crib had been in Mary Catherine's room. Brett hadn't had his own room until Mary Catherine's older brother moved out.

When Caro and Max reached the bottom of the steps and were in the foyer by the front door, the unwanted reality of the situation continued to buzz in Caro's brain, and everything she felt kissing Max suddenly became foolish, stupid, inconsequential.

She turned to Max. "I think I better go."

He didn't say anything, only studied her, and Caro barely breathed because she knew he knew why she was uncomfortable. He realized that somewhere between the kiss on the couch and the lessons in the nursery, she had remembered his past. Ten minutes before, Caro had genuinely believed that if he only took responsibility for Brett it would make everything better, but now she wasn't sure it would. How did a person make up for fourteen years of misery?

She turned, grabbed the doorknob and let herself out before Max could say something that might mitigate her feelings, or kiss her and make her forget everything altogether.

And Max let her go because he knew why she was leaving, even if Caro didn't fully understand it yet. The bottom line to the situation with Mary Catherine wasn't that Max hadn't done his duty by a girl he was supposed to love. Nope. The real issue was that Max had deserted a child and that branded him as untrustworthy. Caro might like him, but she would never trust him.

No woman from Wilburn ever would.

Chapter Five

The minute Caro was safely behind the closed door of her bedroom, she dialed the number for Sadie Senior's cell phone.

When her aunt answered, Caro said simply, "I want you to hire someone else to help Max Riley."

Aunt Sadie laughed. "Caro? Why aren't you talking to your parents about this?"

Realizing the situation with Max had her so stressed she had forgotten her aunt was in the hospital, Caro groaned. "Oh, God, I'm sorry."

"You didn't remember I was in the hospital, did you?"

"No."

"That's okay. For a few seconds there it felt

good to have somebody treating me normally. Now, go talk to your parents about this.''

Caro grimaced. "I can't. But don't worry about it. I'll think of something."

"What did Max Riley do that's so bad you can't discuss it with your parents?"

"Nothing. He didn't *do* anything."

"I'm just about positive I know the answer to this question," Sadie said, and Caro could picture her shrewd smile when she said it. "But, if he didn't *do* anything, why do you need someone else to take over his training?"

Caro didn't hesitate in replying truthfully. Aside from the fact that her aunt probably had already guessed the reason, Sadie was the person in whom Caro and her siblings always confided when they had trouble. "I'm attracted to him."

"Ahhhh," Sadie said through a chuckle. "Part of me doesn't blame you."

"Gee, thanks for helping me figure out how to handle this."

"Caro, sweetie, a woman would have to be dead not to be attracted to him. You shouldn't be embarrassed if he doesn't return the feeling."

"That's the trouble. He does return it."

"Oh," Sadie said curiously. "Then this becomes an entirely different problem."

"My thought exactly."

Sadie laughed. "I don't think we're talking about the same problem. I'm talking about two people falling victim to the oldest aphrodisiac in the book. A baby."

Confused, Caro stared at the phone. "What?"

"Caro, you could be attracted to Max because he's a man in need as much as Max could be attracted to you because you're the woman helping him. I don't think this is a serious problem."

"Oh."

"You're disappointed?"

That was the confusing part. The fact that this could be a simple ploy of nature and not a real attraction should be her easy way out. Instead, it disappointed her and bewildered her. That was the way everything was with Max. Just thinking about Brett tonight had upset her to the point that she had to leave. Yet, on the walk home she'd regretted it.

She wasn't supposed to like him. She wasn't supposed to want to make love with him, to raise Bethany with him, to have babies of her own with him, but she did. After only a few days she had an intense urge to spend the rest of her life with a man she hardly knew. A man with a questionable reputation. It didn't make sense. Yet she wanted it. She wanted *him* in her life.

"He's actually very nice."

"Yes. He is. And wouldn't it be a shame if you let him get away because of a fourteen-year-old mistake."

Sadie's comment and attitude surprised Caro so much that she answered without thinking. "I don't think it's appropriate to call Brett a mistake."

"And I don't think any of us has the right to judge Max, because I don't think any of us knows the whole story."

"It doesn't matter anyway." Dejected and confused, Caro fell to her bed and bounced back on the fat pink satin-ruffled pillow. "The situation with Mary Catherine and Brett is none of my business, if Max and I are just...you know... falling for each other because of Bethany."

"Actually, there's an easy way to test out whether you and Max are getting real feelings for each other or if you're being drawn together by the baby." Sadie paused a heartbeat then said, "Do you want to test it out?"

"That depends on the test."

"The test is continuing to help him with Bethany, but with ground rules. Tell him you want to be sure you're attracted to each other for the right reasons and not just because of Bethany, so you want to have a strictly platonic relationship for a while. Then only see him in his single-dad lessons, where there are other people around so you're forced to act like a teacher and student.''

''I can't do that. Because there is no class for men with infants, his lessons are at his house... where we're always alone.''

''With too much temptation and opportunity,'' Sadie astutely guessed. ''No wonder you guys are crossing lines. Caro, you've got to get him into one of the classes.''

''But we don't have any baby classes.''

''We have a toddler class, young lady,'' Sadie said, scolding her. ''That's good enough.''

''Yes, ma'am.''

Clearly peeved that Caro had questioned her, Sadie continued, ''I'm going to give you instructions and I want you to follow them to the letter. You got me?''

''Yes, ma'am.''

''Okay. Do a home visit tomorrow. In fact, start out by checking his morning routine. Pay close attention to what he's doing with Bethany and fix what needs to be fixed, teach what needs to be taught, and then enroll him in the toddler class where you can get to know each other as people. If the spark's still there after the typical two-week session, then the Mary Catherine situation *is* your business and you have no choice but to ask him about it. But if it turns out there is no spark, you saved yourself and Max a lot of needless worry.''

After that, Sadie began to sound tired and Caro sadly ended the call, praying the doctors would discover her aunt's illness and treat her. Not just so that Sadie could come home, but because Caro, like her parents, was genuinely concerned that something terrible was wrong.

At a quarter to six the next morning, Caro strode up the walk to Max's grandfather's house and rang the bell. A few seconds later, Max answered the door with half-opened eyes and sleep-tousled hair and wearing only sweatpants. His chest and arms were well muscled, a clear indication that the FBI required that he stay in tip-top shape. Black hair dusted his chest and formed an arrow that pointed below the waistband of his gray sweats. Just looking at him made Caro's breath catch. If she hadn't had her long talk with Aunt Sadie the night before, she would have swooned at his feet.

''Caro?'' he said groggily, his voice deep and sexy from slumber. ''What are you doing here?''

''Aunt Sadie told me last night that I had to check your morning routine with Bethany,'' she said, stepping into the foyer, though he hadn't yet invited her.

"Oh." Obviously still half-asleep, he looked at her through narrowed eyelids. "She did?"

"Yes. She told me to see what you were doing wrong on an infant level, and show you how to fix it, and then get you into one of the toddler classes at the single-dad school."

Recognizing there must be a reason behind the abrupt change in his regimen seemed to make him wide awake, because Max straightened and crossed his arms on his chest. "Why would your sick aunt suddenly get involved with my training?"

"I was very confused after I left here last night, and I accidentally called her." She drew a long breath, hoping the advice Sadie had given her was right, because if it wasn't she was about to make a colossal fool of herself. "You're a very attractive man, Max. Any woman would be bowled over by your looks alone. You probably share chemistry with every female on the planet. But more than that, caring for Bethany puts us *both* in a position of liking each other for all the wrong reasons."

"And this pertains to my lessons because..."

"Because we haven't known each other long enough to say for sure we would get along in the real world, let alone be friends, let alone think of each other in the context of something more.

Which is where we were headed last night and why I ran out.'' She took a quick gulp of air for courage and plunged on before he could stop her. ''I was afraid of all the consequences of getting involved with you and I didn't want to have to see you again, so I called Sadie to get myself replaced.

''But she didn't replace me. She told me we should test what we feel about each other. She thinks if we back off, and go through your lessons normally to see if we really do get along as well as we think we do, that would help us to determine if our feelings are real. If we discover we like each other as people and want something more, then we'll cross all those problematic bridges that scared me last night. But if we find out we can't even be friends, then we've saved ourselves a good bit of trouble.''

She watched as Max digested all that. Finally he sighed and said, ''You're right.''

Caro grimaced. ''Aunt Sadie is right.''

''Yeah,'' he said, and rubbed his hand across the back of his neck. ''Your Aunt Sadie is right.''

''Okay, then,'' Caro said, turning toward the steps, because her plans had been explained. There was nothing more to say on that score and it was time to get down to business. ''Is Bethany awake?''

"Not yet, but she will be any minute. She's a six o'clock riser."

"That's why I came at this time. Babies like schedules. Bethany wasn't awake when I left your house the night I stayed over. So I knew if I got here before six I would be here when she woke." She paused on the steps and faced Max. "Actually, the time difference between Pennsylvania and Las Vegas might be working in your favor. Her wake-up time for a feeding in Nevada would actually translate to a morning wake-up call here in Pennsylvania."

As they finished their climb up the steps, Bethany began to cry softly.

Max said, "Right on schedule," and led Caro into the nursery. "Good morning, Bethany," he said, reaching into the crib to check her diaper. "Her diaper's wet, but she's not soaked, so what I would normally do is change her diaper, then take her downstairs for cereal. That way, she can smear her breakfast from head to toe and it won't matter because she hasn't had her bath yet."

"Good," Caro said, watching as Max made short order of the diaper and lifted Bethany out of the crib with a kiss.

He left the nursery and Caro followed.

"The Russells gave me a list of her favorite foods and I bought two boxes of baby cereal and

several jars of strained fruit from their sugges-
tions.'' He glanced at Caro. ''When I spoke with
them yesterday morning, they told me to give her
a bite of cereal, then a bite of fruit.''

''The Russells are very good teachers for you.''
She paused, then asked, ''Are they okay without
Bethany?''

He nodded. ''Reasonably, but I think calling
will give them the sense that they're still in touch
with her.'' He smiled. ''They liked it yesterday
when I asked questions.''

''Then we won't make you too smart.''

Max laughed. In the kitchen, he put Bethany
into the infant seat, which he had set on the table.
After she was strapped in, he prepared the cereal
and opened the fruit. Caro noted that he had the
appropriate baby silverware, undoubtedly provided by the Russells.

Because he spoke to Bethany as he fed her,
Caro said nothing, observing the exchange between the big handsome man and the adorable
little girl. And Sadie's theory echoed in her head.
It would be impossible for a woman not to fall in
love with a gorgeous man who cared so well for
a baby. Max hadn't changed his clothes, put on a
shirt or made coffee. His first concern was for
Bethany and it was touching. Endearing. And
dangerous for a woman who absolutely loved

children and who would idolize any man who so completely put his child's needs before his own.

When Bethany's breakfast was eaten, Max took her upstairs, bathed her and dressed her in a one-piece romper before he carried her to the rocker to feed her a bottle. She fell asleep in his arms and he put her in the crib again.

"She'll sleep for another two hours."

"Uh-huh," Caro said with a laugh. "I think what we have here is a little girl with a three o'clock feeding that translates to your wake-up time here in Pennsylvania. You are a lucky man."

Max laughed. "I know." He led Caro down the stairs and into the kitchen again. "Coffee?"

"I would love some."

"How about breakfast?"

"No, I can't stay that long, but we do need to talk."

Max turned to the counter and pulled the empty coffeepot from the warmer, but from his next words Caro could tell he wasn't as confident as he was trying to appear. "So what did I do wrong in the morning routine?"

"Nothing. You did great. You're a wonderful dad," she said, reassuring him, and he turned and smiled at her. His beautiful blue eyes softened with appreciation, but his mouth curved upward sensually.

Every nerve ending in Caro's body crackled to life, and she realized this was exactly what Sadie was talking about. Caro needed to compliment Max on his abilities with Bethany to keep his confidence high so he would continue to make progress. But in the same way that his smile of thanks sent her senses into overdrive, as if he had smiled at her personally not as his teacher, her compliments to him could be interpreted as her personal feelings for him, and give him the impression that she liked him.

But that wasn't a complete misinterpretation, because she did like him. He was so good with Bethany it was hard not to form the conclusion that he was a basically good person. When she added his looks and charm into the equation, he was a very difficult man to resist. The whole situation was like a vicious cycle that had no real beginning and no clear end, and she understood why Sadie had told her she and Max needed to see each other in class in a setting that was neither private nor personal.

"And that's the point," Caro continued. "You handle her typical routine beautifully. There's no reason for me to come by anymore."

"Oh. Okay." Obviously disappointed, he returned his attention to making coffee.

"But there are lots of reasons for you to begin taking actual classes at the single-dad school."

"I thought you told me there were no classes."

"There are no *infant* classes. But I don't think you need them. What Sadie suggested was that you become part of the toddler class, and after watching you this morning I agree."

"But Bethany's a baby not a toddler."

"The toddler class teaches the beginnings of discipline. The art of the time-out, the word *no* and positive reinforcement."

Max laughed. "Sounds fascinating."

"Hey, if you learn these techniques, you'll know them when you need them and you will be writing Aunt Sadie a thank-you note."

"Okay, I'll trust your advice on this one. When do they start?"

"The new class begins this afternoon at one-thirty. It's a small group. Two divorced dads and one guy whose wife says he's all thumbs with their little boy. Even though he's not single, she's insisting that he get trained by a professional so she's sending him to the single-dad school. I'm guessing the guy is in need of serious help. Just to see him with his son ought to be worth the price of admission."

Max laughed.

"Okay," Caro said, and rose from her seat at the table. "I'll see you this afternoon."

"Don't you want your coffee?"

Caro shook her head. "No. Not now. There's no reason for me to wait around. We did everything we needed to do. I'll see you at one-thirty."

When she was out of his cozy kitchen, Caro let her breath out on a long sigh. Though she hadn't thought it possible, she and Max had held a typical baby session followed by the usual type of postevent discussion. Now all they had to do was get through single-dad classes like a teacher and student, and they might finally find their way to interacting normally.

After that, let the chips fall where they may.

Holding Bethany on the crook of his arm, Max walked into the playroom of Sadie's day care then stopped abruptly. Though he was sure Caro had told him there were to be three other men in this single-dad class, only two dads sat with toddlers on the brightly colored carpets in the center of the playroom floor. But that was good. With every day that passed, his stay in Wilburn grew increasingly difficult. More people remembered who he was, more people remembered the gossip, and it was getting harder and harder to do even simple things like go to the store without having someone grace him with a condemning glare. As far as Max was concerned, the fewer potentially critical Wilburn residents in this class, the better.

Standing in the doorway, studying the two men and toddlers, Max noticed something else, something better. He guessed the kids' ages to be around eighteen months to two years old, but more than that he guessed the ages of the dads to be twenty-two or twenty-three. Which meant there was a good possibility they didn't know who he was. They might not have even heard the rumors.

Just then, Caro looked up from her paperwork and saw him. "Hi," she said, and turned her attention to the two men on the floor with the toddlers. "Hey, everybody, this is Max and Bethany."

"Hi, Max. Hi, Bethany," the first father said. From the pretzel he formed sitting cross-legged on the fuzzy carpet, Max could tell that the man was tall and thin. Though he had bright-red hair, his little boy had dark hair and dark eyes. Dressed in denim shorts and a T-shirt that read I'm the Boss, the stocky toddler looked about ten times tougher than his father.

As Max walked into the room, the dad cheerfully said, "Jeremy, say hi to Bethany," but the little boy just glared at his father, and Max suspected the shirt was correct. Jeremy *was* the boss.

"That's Todd and Jeremy," Caro supplied.

The boss's dad rose for the introduction and Max reached out to shake his hand. "You must be the dad having trouble with his son."

Todd grimaced. "That would be me."

"And this is Will McCoy and his daughter, Addy," Caro said as the second man rose.

"Nice to meet you," Max said, shaking hands with Will. Though Will carried Addy, the little girl was obviously the older of the two children in attendance. Shy and feminine, Addy wore a pink dress with a lace-ruffle hem, black Mary Janes and white socks.

"I'm divorced," Will said, glancing nervously at Caro, causing Max to realize Addy's dad was every bit as shy as Addy. "I don't get a lot of time with Addy and the time I do get I spend just keeping up with her." The little girl timidly nestled into his shoulder, directly contradicting Will's next statement. "She's a hellion."

Caro laughed. "Everybody's here for a good reason," she said, motioning for the fathers and children to take their positions on the carpets again.

Two weeks ago Max would have balked at sitting on the floor, but he had been on the floor plenty of times lately, and without a second thought, he lowered himself and Bethany to the available fuzzy carpet. So much about his life had changed that he was starting to feel he didn't know who he was anymore. But he did know he liked Caro Evans as more than a teacher, and if he actually had to attend a class to prove that, then so be it.

"Now that the introductions are out of the way, I think the first topic we need to tackle is getting our children to do what we want them to do, when we want them to do it." Caro glanced apologetically at Max. "Bethany isn't going to be able to participate in the exercises, but if you watch the other two children, you will see the principles in action."

Max nodded and the class began. Though he initially felt out of place with a child too young to do the activities, he soon became caught up in watching Caro. As the afternoon progressed, he saw her take two shaky dads and begin the process of turning them into baby dynamos—mostly by giving them confidence. It was clear that Caro was a gifted teacher. Someone so good, her students didn't even realize she was guiding them.

Walking home, Max realized that maybe her Aunt Sadie was right. Though he had the Russells and his own parents to call upon for help, it was

Caro who was actually *with* him, helping him adjust from being a single man to being a single parent. And not only did he appreciate it, but also he was afraid to lose her. He didn't think either of those had anything to do with their chemistry. But he did know that fear of losing Caro's assistance with his baby could be what was taking their chemistry and turning it into a desire for something more. Something permanent.

So, as Caro's aunt suggested, he decided to do the entire two weeks of single-dad lessons. But he also spent every other day of the next two weeks on the phone with his parents discouraging them from driving up from Florida to meet Bethany. If Caro Evans was the woman of his dreams, the perfect mate every man dreamed about, and not just a teacher so skillful he was being blinded to her real role in his life, then he owed it to himself to find out. And he wouldn't find out with his parents looking over his shoulder, intimidating Caro more than she was already intimidated by his questionable past and the confusion of their places in each other's lives.

At the end of the final session, after working with Caro and the two other fathers, Max suddenly realized that he was smart enough and now educated enough that he could raise Bethany. Alone, if need be. And just as spontaneously as he came to that conclusion, what he felt for Caro took on a new perspective. He didn't need her for a teacher anymore. He didn't *need* her help. But he still wanted her. She was a beautiful, intelligent woman. Sexy, charismatic, sweet. If he let her get away while he pussyfooted around further analyzing his feelings, he was a crazy man.

"So," he said, sidling up to Caro who stood by the computer in the corner of the day-care playroom. He shifted Bethany to his opposite arm so that she was no longer between him and Caro, a sort of physical symbol that she was no longer their connection. "Are you doing anything tonight?"

Caro peeked up at him but she continued to input information into the computer, creating a certificate for Todd, whose wife was so thrilled with his new baby's abilities that she wanted something to frame.

"Aren't you already over the amount of time you were supposed to stay in Wilburn?"

"I got an extension on my leave of absence. I'm here for another month. It's very hard to clear out an attic, garage and basement, plus paint and do repair jobs, at the same time that you're caring for a baby and attending single-dad school."

"Uh-huh," Caro said. She hit two keys and the printer began to hum. Todd stood by expectantly, so Max wasn't surprised that Caro answered vaguely. "I should have realized that."

"Well, it's okay," Max said, also obscurely, knowing he needed to drag out this part of the conversation as much as he could while Todd was in the vicinity. "I actually appreciated the time-out from my regular routine. I feel like Bethany and I have bonded," he said as Bethany playfully slapped his cheek. "And I'm comfortable that she'll be okay with me no matter where we go."

Caro nodded. "You're probably right." She turned and handed Todd his printed certificate. "Here you are. One certificate ready for framing."

Todd grinned. "Thanks, Caro. I don't know what to say. I'm amazed at how much you taught me. Thanks."

"You're welcome," Caro said. She accepted his awkward, impulsive hug and waved goodbye to Jeremy.

When they were gone, Max tuned to Caro. "There should be an award of some kind for the miracle you performed for those two."

Caro laughed. "Not really. Todd was just nervous. He's relaxed now and Jeremy responds."

"Right," Max said, shaking his head as he laughed. "You, Todd and I know better." He let a second tick off the clock then said, "So, do you want to come by tonight?"

She licked her lips as if stalling, and Max jumped in with, "I'll make you dinner."

She peered at him. "What kind of dinner?"

"How about spaghetti?"

"I like spaghetti."

Because she still seemed to be wavering, Max almost made up an excuse that required her to come to his house to advise him on something to do with Bethany. But after two full weeks of baby training and two full weeks of being nothing but student and teacher, he couldn't think of anything. Plus, he didn't want this to be about Bethany. He wanted this to be a date.

With his free hand, Max caught Caro by the shoulder. "You like spaghetti and I like you. If I had my way I would take you someplace fancy and special, but not only are our options limited here in Wilburn, but also I have to consider Bethany. Spaghetti, wine and a rented movie are the best I have to offer."

To Max's great relief, she smiled. "Okay."

In spite of having a six-month-old baby to contend with, dinner actually went smoothly. At eight, Bethany drank a bottle and fell asleep. Max laid her in the crib, prayed a silent prayer that she would stay sleeping and walked down the steps.

Even though his afternoons had been taken up at single-dad school, he had spent his mornings working in the house, and the entire downstairs was freshly painted and the rugs, drapes and living-room-furniture upholstery had been professionally cleaned. The house smelled better and looked better than it ever had. In fact, Max was beginning to feel very much at home.

"Did you find a movie?"

"Your grandfather had a very odd collection," Caro said, turning to face him when he entered the living room. Though she smiled and held her wineglass as if nothing were amiss, Max could tell she was nervous.

"Was there anything you liked?" Max asked, picking up his own wineglass from the coaster on the shiny coffee table.

"Not unless I get a sudden yen to see John Wayne."

"Oh, my grandfather loved John Wayne," Max said, motioning for Caro to take a seat on the sofa as an unexpected wave of nostalgia about his grandfather swept through him. He rubbed his free hand down his face. "Wow, I feel like it just hit me that he's dead."

"I got odd flashes like that when my grandmother died," Caro said as Max sat on the sofa next to her. "My grandfather passed on before I could really get to know him, but I knew my grandmother very well. With my grandfather gone, she was lonely, so Hannah and I spent many afternoons at her house playing board games or cards, and in general entertaining her. It took me a year to get out of the habit of wanting to stop by to see her.''

With that topic spent, they lapsed into silence, and after a minute or so, Caro said, ''The house looks great.''

''Yeah. But I still have a way to go. I painted and had the house professionally cleaned first because I wanted Bethany to be more comfortable. Which means I saved the hard parts for last.''

''The attic?''

He nodded. ''Attic, basement and garage.''

''I don't envy you!''

''I don't envy me, either.''

Another thirty seconds passed in awkward silence, then Caro pretended to review the movie collection again. Max almost panicked. He wanted to ask her a million questions about her life and her work, but because she hadn't volunteered anything, he worried that questions would appear intrusive. He considered telling her about himself, but didn't want her to think he was self-centered and self-interested. Because all the rules about dating her seemed to be different, Max found himself confused into silence.

When the phone rang, Max was grateful for the interruption. He couldn't believe Caro was so quiet, so nervous. He wished she would talk about teaching, her family, her dog, *anything,* but she had hardly said a word all night, and he had to wonder if her Aunt Sadie's wisdom hadn't been correct. Caro had only been falling for him because of Bethany. Every fiber in Max's being rebelled against the idea. Yet he couldn't discount the obvious. Caro wasn't comfortable with him.

He reached over and grabbed the phone. "Hello... Oh, Mom!" He put his hand over the receiver and faced Caro. "It's my mother. This will be ten minutes tops. Why don't you channel graze for something we can watch."

Caro nodded and picked up the remote, but on second thought set it back down again and took her wineglass into the kitchen.

Telling herself to stop being silly and nervous, she rinsed the stemmed glass, then set it in the dish drainer, but she couldn't stop the thoughts that were racing around in her head.

He didn't like her. Though he had said he did, his behavior tonight indicated otherwise, and Aunt Sadie had been correct. Bethany had brought them together. Bethany made them want to stay together. After a few weeks of getting to know each other as people, and now that he could care for Bethany on his own, Max wasn't attracted to her.

The more Caro thought about it, the more humiliated she felt. It didn't help to remind herself that he had invited her to dinner, because dinner had been strained. Conversation had been non-existent or about Bethany. He was uncomfortable. She felt as if she could crawl out of her skin. And it was time she faced the ugly truth. They had done what Sadie suggested and given themselves time to get to know each other, but rather than cement their relationship, it had merely proved they had nothing in common.

Well, not really *nothing,* Caro thought as tears filled her eyes. She liked Max. She liked him a lot. She wished he had talked about the FBI, or living in Maryland, or anything, absolutely anything personal, because she was interested in him and curious about him. But he hadn't seen fit to tell her anything about himself or his life, and now it was time for Caro to realize she had lost. With Max on the phone, she could slip out unnoticed, and tomorrow when she was more objective she would call him and they could talk about how Sadie had been right. They weren't made for each other.

But there was plenty of time for that tomorrow. Right now she wanted to go home and cry.

She grabbed her purse from the chair by the kitchen table and nearly made it to the back door before she heard Max say, "Caro? Where are you going?"

By now her eyes were brimming with tears. Darn it! Not only did she feel like a fool, she also looked like a fool. Unfortunately, it was too late to change that, so the best thing to do was turn around and have tomorrow's discussion today.

"Look, Max," she said, facing him and praying her tears would shimmer on the edges of her eyelids and not spill over until she was out the door. "I think it's time we admit Aunt Sadie was right. When we take Bethany out of the picture, we don't have a darned thing in common."

"That's only because we haven't talked enough to see if we have anything in common," Max said urgently, rushing to the kitchen door where she stood.

"So why haven't you talked?"

Max combed his fingers through his hair. "Because this is our first date. I didn't want to blow it by sounding like one of those guys who can only talk about himself. Plus, you weren't helping. I got the distinct impression I still scare you to death."

"You don't scare me."

"Good. Because what I really wanted to do all night was this." As he said the last, he dipped his head and whispered his lips against hers. "And this," he added, his tongue lightly tracing the shape of her upper lip. "And this," he said, once again feathering his mouth against hers. "But if you really want to go..."

"No."

"You're sure?" He said the words against her mouth, letting his lips touch hers as he formed each syllable.

"Yes." She paused and pulled away slightly. "But not because you kissed me. I'm staying to give us a chance to talk, since neither of us talked because we were nervous. If I stay, we have to talk."

He frowned. "Really?"

"Yes. We now know we have Bethany and sexual chemistry in common. There has to be more."

"Couldn't we work on understanding the sexual chemistry part tonight?"

"No," she said, but she laughed. Because it felt good to know he still liked her, still wanted her, and because their sense of humor was another thing they had in common. "I want to hear about your job, your life in Maryland, your hobbies."

He sighed elaborately, teasing her again, and Caro smiled at him. "All right, but you're watching John Wayne while we talk."

She rose to her toes and kissed his cheek. "I can handle that."

Because of Bethany, the day care, and the work Max needed to do on the house, they couldn't spend much of the weekend together, but in some ways Max knew that was good. Particularly since the subject of Mary Catherine and Brett had never had a chance to come up. The scant time they had was spent focused on talking about their jobs, college experiences and their families, and Max was feeling very confident about things. So confident, he sneaked into the day care fifteen minutes before the regularly scheduled single-dad class, slid Bethany into an empty play yard and then tiptoed behind Caro who stood by the computer. Because there was no one else around, he grabbed her waist, spun her around and gave her a quick kiss.

She blinked up at him. "You scared the life out of me."

Max gave her a pained look. "That wasn't supposed to scare you."

Caro laughed. "A person can't control her first impulse." She returned to typing entries into a computer worksheet. "What are you doing here?"

"I'm here for class."

Peering at him over her shoulder, she said, "You graduated."

"I didn't get a certificate."

"I'll print up one for you now. You don't have to be here."

"I *want* to be here. Because I was an only child, I don't have any of the knowledge most people got from watching brothers and sisters. Everything I see in this class is something I learn. And everything I learn is a problem I avoid."

"Okay, but I don't think this is the right class for you. I think—" Caro began but she stopped abruptly.

Max noticed a nervous young man standing in the doorway of the playroom. He carried a child who looked to be just exiting the toddler stage. Because the kid was dressed in coveralls and a T-shirt and because he or she had very little hair, Max couldn't even tell if it was a boy or girl.

"Hi."

Caro walked over to meet him. "Hi. I'm Caro Evans. I'll be teaching the single-dad class. And who do we have here?" she asked, tickling the child's chin.

"This is Samantha…Sam," the nervous father said.

"How do you do," Caro said, shaking the little

girl's hand. "If this is Samantha, that means you are…" She glanced at the index card she held in her left hand. "Jim Talbert."

The young man nodded. "Yes. We're here because Samantha's in the terrible twos."

Caro laughed airily. "I see from my notes that neither you nor your ex-wife had trouble with her until her second birthday."

"Yes."

"Well, we'll see what we can do to help Samantha get through this as quickly and happily as possible."

He nodded, and Caro faced Max. She looked confused about what to do with him, so he strode over.

"Hi, I'm Max Riley," he said. "My daughter, Bethany, is in the play yard," he added, pointing to where Bethany sat stacking some blocks.

Jim extended his hand. "Jim Talbert," he said, then he paused as if thinking something through. "Aren't you the Max Riley who played ball with Caro's brother, Luke?"

Max grinned. "One and the same," he said, for the first time since high school feeling comfortable taking the recognition he deserved. "Our team was the one that took State's."

"I know," Jim said, his voice dropping with awe. "You were a legend. But no one's ever seen you. My friends and I thought you died or something.''

"No, I didn't die,'' Max said with a laugh as another father entered the room.

"No, Max Riley didn't die,'' the man said, ambling toward Caro, Jim and Max. "He had a baby with my cousin, Mary Catherine,'' he said. "But he doesn't acknowledge Brett. That's why he doesn't come around Wilburn anymore.''

"And that's not really our concern here in single-dad classes,'' Caro said, jumping in to intervene. "Max, this is Ray Connor and his son, Milo.''

And now Max knew why Caro hadn't wanted him in this class.

"How do you do,'' he said quietly. Trying to get through the uncomfortable situation like a mature adult, he extended his hand to shake Ray's but Ray turned away.

"Let's just get this over with,'' Ray said, clearly annoyed. He walked to the bright carpets in the center of the room, dropped Milo to the floor and fell beside him. "I've heard the drill from friends. My ex-wife insisted I come.'' He glanced at Max. "Now I have even more reason to be sorry I'm here than the ones I had walking in the door.''

As Jim Talbert cautiously ambled to the carpet,

and before Caro could say anything, Max lightly caught her arm. ''Now I see why you didn't want me in this class. But you're also right about something else. I don't need this anymore,'' he whispered as anger resonated through him. After fourteen years he was about as sick of being the bad guy as anybody would be. ''I'm taking Bethany home.''

With that he scooped Bethany out of the play yard, grabbed his diaper bag and strode to the door.

Chapter Six

Max took Bethany to the day care at eight o'clock the next morning. He slid in through the back door and quickly made his way to the office, hoping Caro wasn't yet around or, if she was, that she wouldn't see him.

"So this is Bethany," Lily Evans said, taking the baby from Max's arms. Though Max had been attending single-dad school for two weeks, he had avoided interaction with Caro's parents, afraid of how they would treat him. Since Mary Catherine Connor had been their daughter's best friend as much as Max was their son's, they had undoubtedly been forced to take sides, and Max knew they couldn't have chosen his. Today, however, dealing with them was unavoidable.

Lily kissed Bethany's cheek. "She's adorable!"

"Thanks." Max removed the diaper-bag strap from his shoulder and set the colorful container filled with Bethany's necessities on a convenient counter. "I like to think so."

"You would have to be blind not to think so," Peter Evans said, walking into the office. "How are you, Max?" he asked as he shook Max's hand.

"Not bad," he replied. "I have errands to run this morning and I was wondering if I could leave Bethany at the day care for a few hours."

"Sure," Lily said cheerfully, though her friendliness was more professional than personal and her smile didn't reach her eyes. "You'll be billed hourly and the amount will be added to the total of your single-dad school account."

"Good," Max said amicably, though he was getting angrier and angrier about the predicament he was in. First he was shunned or scorned nearly everywhere he went. Then he couldn't have a regular relationship with Caro. Now he couldn't even behave normally with two people who had been like second parents to him. Worse, they couldn't behave normally with him. They were friendly enough, but in the old days Pete would have given him a jab to the arm. Lily would have kissed his cheek. Neither even considered it now.

"I should be back around noon."

He turned to walk out the door, but as he did he saw Caro standing in the entryway to the playroom and his heart felt as if it stopped. Their gazes caught and held and all of her questions were in her eyes. Why hadn't he returned her calls? Why had he brought Bethany to her parents', rather than to her? Didn't he want her anymore?

Max quickly looked away and strode out onto the gray-painted porch, not even saying hello. Ray Connor's reaction was confirmation that Caro would be ridiculed if anyone even suspected she was becoming romantically involved with Max, so the right thing to do would be to stay away from her. But he had one shot, one final, flimsy shot at fixing this, and though he'd never had reason to take drastic measures before, this morning he did. Then, if it didn't work out, he would walk away. Immediately. He wouldn't contact Caro again.

He marched down the sidewalk, anger gnawing at his insides. Not because he knew in his heart that this wasn't going to work and he was about to lose Caro, but because he was tired. Very, very tired. He strode by his grandfather's house, turned the corner onto Johnson Avenue, immediately ducked under the low branch of an apple tree and then slithered between the tall bushes that had taken him to Mary Catherine Connor's backyard several nights a week when he wasn't supposed to be visiting. Neither one of them had realized that what they were doing fourteen years ago would ripple through the rest of their lives, but it had. And Max couldn't take it anymore.

Using his FBI training, a little wit and a little wisdom, he surveyed the situation hoping to ascertain when she was alone in the house. He saw Brett leave on his bike, then, a few seconds later, he watched Mary Catherine's mother drive off and realized she was probably on her way to the bank where she worked as a teller. When her dad didn't come out, Max began to get nervous until he calculated Dave Connor's age to be sixty-seven, which meant he would probably spend his mornings at the local diner, chatting with other retired men, because that's what the older men in Wilburn did.

Still, Max waited and watched until he was as convinced as he could be that Mary Catherine was alone.

Even as sure as he was, he didn't go to the front door. He entered through the garage and maneuvered around an aging Toyota, to the door leading to the kitchen. He grabbed the knob and twisted slowly. It gave easily, and he walked into the blue-and-white kitchen to find Mary Catherine drinking coffee at the breakfast nook.

"This has got to stop."

Startled, she gasped and looked up from the magazine she was reading. Still attractive at age thirty, she didn't need more than her simple red shirt and denim shorts to turn heads. With her brown hair swept up in a bouncy ponytail, she looked more Caro's age than Maria's. And if she really wanted to go out with men, or find a substitute father for Brett, Max knew she could.

The fact that she never did proved she didn't want to.

"Oh, God, Max. You scared the hell out of me."

"That doesn't even begin to balance the scales," he said angrily as he stepped farther into the room. "Mary Catherine, I can't do this for you anymore. I can't lie anymore."

Without as much as an expression of remorse, she returned her gaze to her magazine. "You have to."

"No, I don't. I am not Brett's father…"

"You promised."

"An eighteen-year-old boy promised. This thirty-two-year-old man is telling you that it's time for this to stop.'' He walked to the table, and, to get her attention, he caught her arm, forcing her to look up at him. ''It's time. My God, Mary Catherine, your son has a right to know his real father.''

''If he had any other father, I might agree with you,'' Mary Catherine said. Now as angry as Max, she glared at him. ''It's better that he think he has a father who ignores him than to know his real dad.'' She returned her gaze to the magazine. ''Besides, what difference does it make? You'll be back in D.C. in a few weeks. Now that your grandfather's dead there's no reason for you ever to return to Wilburn. I know you're the talk of the town because of the baby girl you brought home. But before you know it, you'll be leaving again and it won't matter anymore.''

Frustrated, confused, Max sat on one of the chairs beside the round wooden table and decided to appeal to her sense of fair play. ''Mary Catherine, I found somebody that I like.''

She shrugged.

''Somebody I really, really like. Somebody I could actually marry,'' he said, then swallowed hard because he realized it was true. The real problem Max had with Caro Evans wasn't just that he wanted to spend time with her while he was in Wilburn. It was that he wanted her in his life forever. She was sweet, kind and wonderful, and so perfect for him that he knew it in less than a month. "And she's from Wilburn."

"I can't help that."

"Yes, you could. All you have to do is tell people I'm not Brett's father."

She glared at him again. "Do you think it's as easy as that? Do you think I can take out an ad in the *Dispatch* and everything will be okay?"

Max combed his fingers through his hair. "I don't know. But you could start by telling the Evans family the truth."

She shook her head. "No. It's too late for that now. Besides, what I'm doing is working."

"Working for you, Mary Catherine—"

"Damn it, Max! Stop badgering me. I can't change things now. And you know why."

"Yes, I know why," Max said, and resignedly rose from his seat. He could prove that he wasn't Brett's father with a DNA test, but that wasn't the issue. He had made a promise based on circumstances that had changed, but Mary Catherine wasn't letting him out of it. He walked toward the door that led to the garage, about to sneak out the same way he had come in, but Mary Catherine stopped him.

"And, Max," she called. "Don't get any ideas about spreading the truth yourself. Especially not to the Evanses, because I'll not only deny it, I'll call you a liar and I'll make it stick. Everybody believed me the first time and you were a football hero.'' She smiled. ''You were the favorite son. Now that everybody distrusts you, I'm just about certain that I could ruin your life for good in this town.''

''Don't trouble yourself. You already have.''

When Caro showed up at Max's door the next morning, she took him completely by surprise. Because her phone calls had stopped, he thought she finally understood that Ray Connor's reaction was just the tip of the iceberg of what would happen to her if she got involved with him and she was quietly backing out the same way he was.

''Hi,'' she said, stepping into the foyer. ''Hi, Bethany,'' she added as she kissed the cheek of the little girl Max held.

''What's up?'' Max asked carefully, not moving from the door, not inviting her in, though Caro walked past him into the foyer as if nothing was wrong.

''I thought I would take you and Bethany to the mall today.''

She faced Max with a smile, but he could see from the wary expression in her eyes that she was hurt. They had spent time together over the weekend, beginning a personal relationship, yet after the confrontation with Ray Connor two days before, he hadn't said a word to her. The look on her face seemed to say he wasn't getting rid of her so easily. She wanted some explanations.

He couldn't give her any.

"I checked your account. You paid in advance for two more weeks of single-dad lessons. So either you sign up for another class, or we go back to private sessions," she said, holding his gaze.

Max said nothing, but as they stared at each other, the look in her eyes changed from hurt to confident to desirous, and then suddenly her gold-rimmed eyes were smoldering. Her attraction to him was so strong, he felt he could reach out and touch it.

"But even if you choose another class, you've already missed two meetings, so I thought we would use this morning to make up the time by going to the mall to buy a high chair."

Her fiery brown eyes continued to hold his gaze, and Max finally understood what she was telling him. She recognized that the run-in with Ray Connor had virtually sent Max into hiding and because he wouldn't talk about it, she seemed to realize he *couldn't* talk about it. But she wanted to be with him, so she used the single-dad school as a reason for them to be together. She liked him

enough and was attracted to him enough that for
at least the time being she would forgo explanations for the opportunity to be with him.

For the second time that morning, she surprised
him, but this time she shocked him into silence.
A chance from her, the benefit of the doubt from
her, was really the only thing he wanted. He
didn't give a damn what the rest of the people in
this town thought, though he did know that if
word of their romance leaked, Caro's life
wouldn't be easy. But with the single-dad school
as a cover, there was no way anyone would find
out. Plus, their problems only existed in Wilburn.
Out of this town—like twenty miles away at the
mall—they could do anything they wanted.

"Okay," he said, turning to walk up the stairs
to go to the nursery. "Should we dress Bethany
up for her big trip?"

"Sure. Why not? I packed some really adorable
outfits that I found in the Russells' closet," she
said, following Max up the stairs as he had hoped
she would. "We'll make her the belle of the mall.
That's half the fun of having a baby girl."

Max scowled over his shoulder. "Maybe for
you."

She laughed. "You better get used to it, because she's going to want to dress up for school,

and you're the only person who can make her look cute.''

Not if I can help it, Max thought. He didn't know how he was going to do it, but somehow Caro would be returning to Maryland with him. This time next year she would be buying Bethany's outfits and warming his bed. In the same way that Aunt Sadie's plan to force Caro and Max into a platonic relationship had helped them to see they weren't merely interested in each other because of Bethany, the conversation he had had with Mary Catherine forced him to see he already loved Caro. He wasn't being driven by hormones. He wasn't overwhelmed by her unexpected kindness or her innate goodness. It was a combination of all of them. It was a combination that added up to love, commitment, forever. And Max wanted it. In Maryland, they could have it.

He didn't know how he was going to get her to move away with him. He honest to God had no clue how he would get her to fall in love with him in spite of the fact that he appeared to have a fatal flaw. But somehow he was going to get her to see beyond the town's distrust of him and marry him.

They dressed Bethany in a little blue sundress with a matching bonnet, white socks with a rim of rippling lace and white sandals. Then, in the kitchen, as Max shoved new disposable diapers into the diaper bag, Caro filled a juice bottle and a water bottle.

"We'll take an empty spare just in case she wants milk for lunch."

Max interpreted that as meaning they were having lunch together, so he didn't argue. But also, he watched her look right at the high chair he had bought the day before without really seeing it, almost as if her subconscious wouldn't let her recognize that they had no "single-dad school" reason to be together that morning. Another proof, in Max's eyes, that she wanted this time with him as much as he wanted this time with her.

Stifling a laugh, he said, "Great." Then he scooped up Bethany and led Caro to his SUV.

"So, how's your aunt?" he asked as he maneuvered his vehicle out of the driveway.

"It's a funny thing about being sick," Caro replied. She finished buckling her seat belt, then shifted to face him. "You go to the doctor because you're too tired to work and he orders tests that don't actually get done until two weeks later. If there's something really wrong with you, you could die before they find it."

"I think if there was something serious enough to cause a doctor to worry, he would speed up the tests."

Caro sighed. "I know, but he isn't. And he also isn't releasing her from the hospital, yet her insurance isn't arguing about picking up the tab."

"That means there's a good reason she's there."

"I know."

The fear in her voice finally penetrated Max's thinking. "I get it. You think she's sicker than everybody's telling you." He glanced over at her. "And you're scared."

"Yeah."

"Okay, here's the deal. You're upset because of a situation you can't control with your aunt and I'm angry because of a circumstance beyond my control. So what we're going to do is forget all our troubles and just have some fun at the mall."

She returned his smile. "Good idea."

He sighed. "Caro, that was supposed to make you laugh, because men can't have a good time at a shopping mall."

"Oh," she said, then she did laugh. "I get it."

"Good," he said, very pleased that he could make her laugh but even more pleased that he understood her, because that confirmed what he believed. He loved her. What he was doing wasn't selfish. It was right.

When they reached the mall, Max immediately took care of getting Bethany out of her car seat.

Caro rummaged in the back of the SUV for the diaper bag and the fold-up stroller.

"You've really got a lot of stuff back there," she said, pushing the stroller to the passenger door where Max stood.

"I never know what I'll need," he said, then slid Bethany into the stroller Caro had waiting. She secured the strap of the seat and Max grabbed the diaper bag and slung it over his shoulder. "Literally. I don't know what she's going to need or when she's going to need it, so I try to have some of everything on hand."

"Well, you could probably do without half the clothes," Caro said as they walked toward the mall entrance, Max wheeling the baby in front of them.

"Probably."

"I also think you could get rid of all the toys except Mr. Bunny, of course, since that's her favorite."

Caro held open the glass door for Max. "So, where do you want to look for a high chair?"

Max pushed Bethany into the air-conditioned mall, intending to buy another high chair if that was what it took to keep Caro in his company. But it suddenly occurred to him that the lie he had agreed to for Mary Catherine's sake was what had gotten him into this predicament in the first place and he couldn't lie anymore. Because there were so many things he had to keep a secret, he couldn't so much as stretch the truth about anything else.

He drew a quick breath. "I wasn't going to tell you this, but I bought a high chair yesterday."

"You did?"

"Yes. That's one of the reasons I left Bethany at the day care."

"Oh."

He stopped pushing the stroller and put his hand on Caro's upper arm. Though he appreciated that she had used the single-dad school as an excuse to be with him that morning, he knew there couldn't be any more pretense. He needed to be honest with her, but more than that he needed her to be honest with him. "I really just wanted to spend the day with you."

"Oh," Caro said, then, as if realizing he was stopping the pretense so they could relax, she smiled at him.

As always when she smiled at him, Max's heart felt as if it stopped. To him she was the most beautiful woman on the face of the earth. Her smile could charm the angels, but her eyes really were the windows to her soul. They could be as warm as coffee, or as hot as smoldering coals. Within seconds the expression in her eyes could take him from feeling the warmth of acceptance to the heat of desire. And right now the temperature of the electric current arcing between them was so high, he was amazed it didn't start a small fire.

"I really just wanted to spend the day with you, too," she admitted softly, then she glanced around, breaking the spell. "So, if you've already got a high chair, where do you want to go? What do you want to do?"

"I don't know," he said, relief rippling through him. He couldn't do anything about the way the look in her eyes made him want to make love to her for hours. Neither one of them was ready. But spending the day together was a good start toward getting her to see that what they felt was right and good, and that was the first step toward getting her to move away with him. "Why don't you tell me?"

"We could go to the baby department of a big store and look around. I could explain a few things to you."

"That's an idea," Max said, trying not to make a big deal out of what they were doing, but it was. This was the stuff real love was made of, common, ordinary, day-to-day details, and that's what he wanted from Caro. Real love. He steered them in the direction of the first department store he saw. Caro walked beside him. In her stroller, Bethany chewed a teething ring. Max felt as if his life had settled.

Now all he had to do was figure out how to keep Caro in his life forever. Without lying. Without giving away Mary Catherine's secret. Without hurting Brett. And without ripping Caro away from her own family.

Yeah, right.

After a morning of examining baby equipment that somehow led to an hour of comparative shopping for hockey sticks, shin guards and elbow pads because Max played on an intramural ice hockey team, Caro wasn't even the slightest bit bored or tired. More important, she wasn't the slightest bit uncomfortable. She didn't want to get away. She didn't feel she needed a minute to regroup. She was perfectly happy with Bethany and Max. She was glad she had missed Max enough in the time they were apart to realize she didn't want to lose him—as Aunt Sadie had said—because of a fourteen-year-old mistake. Which meant she had to go back to her original plan of getting him to bring Brett into his life so she and Max could have a real relationship.

But she also knew the only way to convince Max that it was possible to fix the mistake he'd made when he was too young to know better was through complete honesty. Max had started it with his admission about the high chair and wanting to spend the day with her, and though there were certain subjects they couldn't yet broach, Caro knew they had to keep the honesty going.

So, when lunch was almost over, and she and Max were about as happy as any two people could be, she didn't stop herself from saying what she felt.

"You know, I like you so much it's almost scary."

Max peered up from his ham and cheese sandwich. "You think it's scary to you? You should be me."

Because that shed some light onto why he'd virtually gone into hiding after he'd run into Ray Connor but didn't actually explain it, Caro asked, "What do you mean?"

"FBI agents aren't supposed to get weak-kneed. Especially not at just *seeing* little blondes."

That made her laugh. "You get weak-kneed just seeing me?" she asked, then she laughed again. "Things are going much better for me than I thought."

Max only stared at her. "This isn't funny. You make me crazy and it scares me because I feel like I'm getting accustomed to something I can't have.'' He paused and caught her gaze again. ''But I want it anyway. And I'm probably going to pursue it.''

Excitement rippled through her. He felt the same way she did, except she had hope. Eventually she would get him to see that becoming part of Brett's life was the right thing to do and then everything would be okay.

''So you're warning me.''

Max didn't hesitate. ''Yes. I'm warning you.''

''Okay,'' she said, not quite sure why he felt she had to be *warned* but glad they continued to be completely honest. She nodded in the direction of the stroller. ''Bethany's sleeping.''

After checking Bethany, Max glanced at Caro across the table. Remorse filled his beautiful blue eyes. ''We better go.''

She didn't think leaving the mall was the end of the world, though she thought it was another good sign that he wasn't yet ready for their day to end. She smiled at him. ''Yeah. Let's go.''

Before she could stand, however, Max grabbed her hand and stopped her. ''Come home with me?''

The serious expression in his eyes reminded her of just how hopeless he felt. But, in a way, that was good. There was nothing like pain to get somebody in the mood for advice on how to fix things. Which meant she had to tell him about her plan with Brett this afternoon, while he would be receptive.

She smiled at him. "Okay."

"Stay for dinner?"

That made her laugh. "We just ate."

"We'll still need to eat again later," he said, rising. He paid the bill at the counter by the door and strolled Bethany out of the restaurant.

Comfortable and happy, Caro looped her arm through his as they headed for the mall exit. "You're just trying to get me to commit to spending five more hours with you."

"Probably." He pushed the stroller outside when Caro held the door open for him. "Does that bother you?"

"No," she said, not just because she needed the chance to talk about Brett, but because she liked being with Max. Actually, she loved being with him. The truth was, she was beginning to suspect she was either already in love with him or darned close. He was good. He was kind. He was strong and smart and sexy. He was everything she had ever looked for in a mate. The only problem was getting him to acknowledge Brett and she had a plan for that. As far as Caro was concerned, her life was edging toward perfect, and with one small push from her it would be perfect.

Max lifted Bethany out of the stroller and put her into her car seat, then began to fasten her in. Caro wheeled the stroller to the back of the SUV, opened the hatch and slid it inside. She slammed the door and walked along the passenger side to where Max had just finished settling the baby.

With Bethany secure and happy, Max smiled at Caro as she approached him. When she was close enough, he caught her upper arms, pulled her to him, and bent his head and kissed her. Spontaneously, deliciously, his soft, smooth lips skimmed across hers, and no thought of resisting entered Caro's brain. Particularly not when he tasted so right, so perfect. Her arms slid around his neck. His slid around her waist, pulling her closer to him. Their bodies pressed together intimately. In the hot sun, in an open parking lot, he kissed her deeply, passionately, and Caro fell that last step over the line.

She loved him.

She knew she loved him.

He released her and whispered, "Let's go home."

As Max rounded the hood of the SUV to get to the driver's side, he caught a glimpse of the entry to the mall and there stood Mary Catherine Connor staring at him. It was clear she had seen him kiss Caro, and Max froze as a truly insidious thought struck him. Bethany's mother might have been strong-willed and independent, but she had always been that way. Mary Catherine started off sweet, but after her unplanned pregnancy she had become ruthless.

For the first time Max could remember, his blood ran cold. Not because he was afraid Mary Catherine would hurt him, but because Mary Catherine could hurt Caro. She wasn't merely capable. If she thought Max and Caro were getting too close, she would see it as a necessity to protect her secret. After all, people falling in love were supposed to tell each other everything, and if he and Caro started to date in earnest, Mary Catherine would assume he would confess to Caro that he wasn't Brett's father. Then, like Max, Caro would become a potential weak spot in the lie, and Mary Catherine would have to discredit her. Mary Catherine would believe that ruining Caro's name was a necessity to protect herself and Brett.

With his eyes locked with Mary Catherine's, Max knew she was telling him that if he continued to see Caro, she would do whatever she had to do to keep her secret safe.

* * *

Max was quiet on the drive home. He couldn't believe he had been so shortsighted that he didn't realize Mary Catherine would hurt Caro. Worse, he couldn't believe he had no clout or position to fight her. He couldn't use a DNA test because he didn't necessarily want to expose her lie. For all its other faults, Mary Catherine's lie was intended to protect Brett, and it did. Which was proof that Mary Catherine would do whatever it took to protect her son. If she set out to ruin Caro's reputation, she would. And because Max had made a promise to keep her secret, to backhandedly validate her lie by never refuting it, he couldn't use the truth to stop her if she went after Caro. His only rescue was to get away from Caro, so Mary Catherine would stop seeing her as a threat.

After putting Bethany down for a nap, Max suggested he and Caro go to the backyard to clean out his grandfather's flower beds. He couldn't very well ask her to leave ten minutes after he had all but begged her to come home with him, but he did have to figure out how to get her out of his life before Mary Catherine considered her a threat and did something.

"Did you love Mary Catherine?" Caro asked suddenly.

"Yes," Max confessed, though he didn't look up at her. He kept digging, loosening the soil around a rhododendron bush, hoping a show of disinterest might cause her to think he had changed his mind about a relationship with her.

"But?"

Max looked up at her. "But what?"

"But something happened. Something had to have happened between you and Mary Catherine. Or you would have taken responsibility for Brett."

"Yeah. You're right."

He said nothing else and went back to loosening dirt, continuing to try to discourage her.

Caro sighed. "So what happened?"

Still digging, Max said, "Caro, as far as I'm concerned, this is ancient history. But more than that, I made a promise to Mary Catherine that I wouldn't talk about Brett with anyone." For this he caught her gaze. Not only was this the crux of their problem, but also his inability to break a confidence was a deal breaker for a real relationship between him and Caro. If she were from another town, he could tell her the story because she wouldn't know any of the players and her knowledge of the circumstances would be meaningless. But because she was from Wilburn he couldn't breathe a word.

If she were smart, the very fact that he was

keeping a secret should send her scurrying away from him.

"And I won't. I won't discuss this with *anyone*."

Instead of arguing with him, or pointing out that lovers couldn't have secrets, Caro surprised him by asking, "Why would you make a promise like that?"

"At the time it seemed like the right thing to do," Max said, and went back to digging. She would get the message soon enough that if he couldn't be perfectly honest with her, he wouldn't make a good husband. There was no reason to beat the point to death, except to continue to assert that he wouldn't break this promise. "Plus, my silence didn't seem to be a big deal. Both of us believed it wouldn't matter because I was leaving town."

"And you didn't want to have to stay behind?"

Max sighed. "I would have stayed behind. I asked to stay behind. Mary Catherine didn't want me to."

"You've never disputed that this child is yours. You would have stayed behind once you discovered she was pregnant. But she didn't want you to." Caro shook her head. "That doesn't make any sense."

"In case you haven't noticed, Mary Catherine

doesn't always make sense.'' He rose from the rhododendron bush and walked toward the gardening shed. Now that they were getting to the real heart of the matter, Max knew he had to change the subject. Particularly since more things troubled him about this situation than his reputation or Mary Catherine's craziness, and it was getting harder and harder for him to stay on the periphery as she insisted.

Caro scrambled after him. ''Yes, actually, I have noticed that Mary Catherine's life doesn't make sense.''

Two feet from the shed, Max stopped abruptly. He knew he had to end this conversation, but he also suddenly recognized that Caro was the first objective Wilburn resident he had met in fourteen years. A chance like this one might never again come along. And he had already decided to remove himself from Caro's life. So answering a few small questions wouldn't hurt her or get her hurt.

Before he opened the door of the shed, he faced Caro again. ''Is Mary Catherine a good mother?''

''She seems to be.''

''And Brett is happy?''

''I suppose he's as happy as a boy can be without a dad...''

''While living in a small town with a lot of

gossip and speculation,'' Max said, finishing her sentence for her before he blew his breath out on a sigh. He squeezed his eyes shut. ''This whole situation is wrong.''

Knowing he had already said too much, he turned toward the door, but Caro caught his arm and forced him to face her again.

''Then why don't you do something about it?''

Seeing the concern in her eyes, knowing she would be safe as soon as he got out of her life, and refusing to leave this relationship looking like a complete bastard, Max said, ''I tried. Yesterday.''

Her face brightened. ''You did?''

He nodded.

''What happened?''

''Caro, I really shouldn't tell you any more than I already have.''

''Max, we both know you can't get away without telling me anything. You have to tell me at least some of what happened.''

He sighed heavily. ''Actually, Caro, that's the point. I can't tell you anything and we can't have a relationship, not a real one, unless we're honest with each other.''

She stared at him as if he were crazy. ''Why can't you tell me?''

''Because Mary Catherine made me promise to keep this secret and she has her reasons.''

"She's broke, but apparently doesn't want your money. Her child is growing up without a good male influence, but she doesn't want you to spend time with him—though you're his father. And you're telling me she has her reasons, so you just obey?"

"I'm not obeying. I'm keeping a promise I made fourteen years ago."

Obviously exasperated, Caro gaped at him. "What kind of promise?"

"A promise not to talk about the situation."

She groaned. "This is ridiculous."

"Not if you know the whole story. And particularly not to Mary Catherine."

Caro studied him for a few seconds and from the way her expression changed, Max could see she'd come to an unexpected realization.

"You don't agree," she said incredulously. "Whatever the promise is, you wish you hadn't made it."

Recognizing she was perilously close to figuring out the truth, Max said, "Caro, this conversation is over."

"Why?"

"Because I made a promise, and by telling you these bits and pieces, you're very close to guessing the truth. And that's not right. I can't break this promise."

"You're *that* honest?"

"This has nothing to do with honesty. There are consequences attached to my breaking the promise. They affect me, but they affect Mary Catherine, too."

"And what about Brett?"

Max drew a long breath. "They affect Brett most of all."

Caro threw her gardening gloves to the picnic table. "I don't get it."

"That's the point. You're not supposed to get it. No one is. And that's what will keep us from having a relationship. I can't go into a relationship with you knowing I have a secret. You shouldn't want a relationship with me knowing I'm not being completely honest." He shook his head. "This doesn't work. Not at all. Not even in theory. In fact, I think you should go."

"That's the first thing we agree about," she said, and picked up the small shoulder-strap purse she had set on the bench seat of the redwood table.

He watched her storm down the driveway, out to the sidewalk and out of his life, grateful that he had protected her, but overwhelmed with misery. Instinctively he knew he was letting the best thing he'd ever had slip away from him. And there wasn't a damn thing he could do about it.

Chapter Seven

Max didn't attend the single-dad class in which he had enrolled. He also didn't call Caro to explain, because there was nothing to say that she didn't already know. He couldn't be around her without longing for a way to get her into his life forever. Yet marrying her was out of the question. Even if he discounted his fear that Mary Catherine would hurt Caro, no matter how he looked at this, the bottom line continued to be that he couldn't break his confidence, and husbands and wives weren't supposed to have secrets.

No matter how tempting, a relationship between him and Caro wasn't going to happen. Believing he could love and marry her had been a nice dream, but it wasn't a practical reality. He knew that. In a sense, he had known it all along.

What he was doing now was accepting it and resolving to get on with the rest of his life.

But on Sunday morning when he was reminding himself one more time that they had only really known each other a few weeks and he would get beyond the empty feeling that he had every time he thought about returning to Maryland without her, she called him.

"I'm sorry."

Because he was the one who had started their fight, she took Max so much by surprise that he spoke without thinking. "You're sorry? For what?"

"For pushing you about Mary Catherine and making you mad enough that you asked me to leave."

"I didn't ask you to leave because of your questions about Mary Catherine. I asked you to leave because I have a secret. A big secret. The kind of secret that lovers shouldn't have, and because of that I can't get involved with you."

"I understand what you're saying, I just don't happen to agree."

Max squeezed his eyes shut. The optimism in her voice almost did him in, but he knew she was wrong. A man and woman couldn't have a relationship unless they were completely honest with each other. He couldn't be completely honest with her.

The awful emptiness in the pit of his stomach grew, but he ignored it.

As if she didn't notice Max hadn't responded, Caro blithely chatted on. "And that's why I called. Because I don't agree with your assessment of our situation, I'm inviting you to lunch."

In spite of the fact that he knew they had no future, her invitation was shockingly tempting. All he wanted was to be with her, to spend time with her, because once he returned to Frederick, he would never see her again. Letting this opportunity slip away seemed horribly wrong.

He was on the verge of accepting, when she said, "At my parents' house with my family."

Like a splash of cold water in the face, that small phrase brought him back to reality. "I don't think so."

"Sadie Junior is in Pittsburgh. Maria and her family are on vacation. That leaves me, Luke, Mom and Dad, and Hannah. I'm sure you can trust me and Luke. You've already had a chat with my parents. And Hannah hasn't bitten anyone in years. Not since that ugly episode in kindergarten."

Though her suggestion was absurd, Max laughed.

"And my parents talked nonstop about Bethany the other day."

"Really?"

"Yes. They think she's adorable." She paused. "Come on, Max. Please."

He knew he should resist her. He knew having lunch with her family was wrong. He knew even hesitating gave her a false impression. But his mouth couldn't seem to form the word *no* any more than it could form the word *yes*.

"Okay, if you won't come for me, come for Luke." She paused, and he heard her say, "Here, Luke. Take the phone."

Max's mouth fell open in disbelief. Before he could think of a decent way to get out of the conversation, Luke was on the line.

"Why in heaven's name would you refuse an invitation to eat my dad's barbecued ribs?"

"Your dad's making barbecued ribs?"

"Yeah, but Caro says you won't come over. My parents just wanted a chance to relax and catch up with your life. It's not a big deal."

Max took the receiver away from his ear and stared at it. For a good ten seconds he wondered if he had misinterpreted Caro's invitation, and in the end decided he must have, because clearly this was a family request, not a personal one from Caro.

He didn't like the idea of being close to Caro and tempting fate, but if he refused Pete Evans's ribs and the opportunity to socialize normally and rekindle his friendship with people who were obviously giving him a second chance, Luke would realize something was wrong and start probing. Plus, Max knew it would be good for him and Bethany to get out. He was tired of hiding. No, what he was tired of was the lie. And in one way, shape or form he had to stop it. He wouldn't say anything to the Evanses that he wasn't allowed to say. He wouldn't even talk about Brett. But if his behavior this afternoon caused the Evanses to see he wasn't a villain, and if that made them begin to wonder if there wasn't something wrong with Mary Catherine's story, then so be it.

"Caro didn't say anything about ribs. For your dad's ribs, Bethany and I will be there. Name the time."

"One o'clock."

"Okay," Max said, and hung up the phone.

Max arrived at Caro's parents' exactly on time. Caro saw him pushing Bethany's stroller up the driveway and walked from behind the house to meet him.

Both she and Max had thought their last visit ended badly, but after a day or two to think about it, Caro realized it had not. Though he had basically told her to butt out because he was bound by a promise he'd made to Mary Catherine, his questions about Mary Catherine's mothering skills and Brett's welfare caused Caro to realize Max regretted more than giving his word. He was worried about Brett. And that one little fact reminded her that their situation was not hopeless.

"Hi!"

"Hi."

Caro understood his less-than-enthusiastic greeting because she knew he felt trapped by his secret. But he really wasn't. Though he had vowed to stay out of Brett's life, Max's need to care for his son and Brett's need of a dad superseded a fourteen-year-old promise. Once Max realized that and got involved with Brett—even if he had to go over Mary Catherine's head by filing for visitation rights—he would be free.

Plus, Caro knew something else Max obviously hadn't yet recognized. The people of Wilburn were too smart to hate him forever without question. Not only had her parents softened toward Max after baby-sitting Bethany at the day care, but also most of the men who took classes with him had come to like him. Because he was a genuinely good person. Eventually, people would begin to see that and begin to wonder about the fourteen-year-old problem. And once the real questions started, it would be Mary Catherine who would be answering them.

As far as Caro was concerned, Max's reputation in Wilburn would soon resolve itself, but in the meantime she had to prevent him from doing something foolish like returning to Maryland, or putting so much time and distance between them that they lost each other.

She reached into the stroller to lift Bethany out. "Hello, little pumpkin head," she said, rubbing noses with Bethany, who giggled. "Don't you look cute today," she added, turning toward the backyard. "Max is here with the baby, Mom," she called as she led Max up the driveway, to the sidewalk beside the garage and to the yard.

Four oak trees marked the boundaries for Caro's parents' property. The branches of the back trees created a leafy canopy that shaded two redwood picnic tables and a grill. A stone walk led from the picnic area to a small patio by the back porch of the two-story redbrick house. Caro had never realized how homey the setup was until she remembered that for the past fourteen years Max had lived in a condo in Florida with his parents, or in a town house in Maryland.

"I had forgotten how great this yard is," he said, glancing around in appreciation.

"Thanks," Caro began, but her mother interrupted her.

"You just give that baby to me!"

As Lily Evans reached out and took the little girl from Caro's arms, Max said, "Hello, Mrs. Evans, thanks for inviting us."

Caro's mother laughed lightly. "We're all adults now, Max. You can call me Lily."

"All right…Lily."

"Help yourself to iced tea," Lily said, her attention taken by rearranging Bethany's T-shirt over her tummy. "Aren't you adorable!"

Seeing her mother was preoccupied, Caro said, "The glasses are by the pitcher."

"Thanks."

"Hey, Max," Luke said as he walked out of the kitchen and across the back porch. "So that's Bethany."

"Yeah. That's Bethany."

"How old is she?"

"Going on seven months," Max said, and Caro watched him stiffen slightly as if he was afraid of where the conversation was going. She prayed a silent prayer that he would just relax and let this happen, because only by easing through these awkward moments would he get comfortable enough for people to accept him.

Luckily, her father came barreling through the

back door and raced down the porch steps. "Oh, hey, Max. Good to have you here," he said as he ran to the grill. He lifted the lid and a steamy burst of fragrance billowed out. "Oh, Lord! Those are some sweet-smelling ribs."

"They sure are," Luke said, sniffing with delight as he walked over to the grill. "What do you think? Another five minutes?"

"Two maybe," Pete said, closing the grill lid. He turned to Max. "So what have you been up to, Max?"

"Not much. Work keeps me very busy."

"Oh," Pete said, setting his barbecue fork on the side of the grill. "That's going to be a problem with a baby."

"I've thought about that."

"Are you going to get a live-in? Something like a nanny?" Lily asked. Holding Bethany, she took a seat on one of the available lawn chairs under a leafy tree, and was comfortably ensconced in cool shade with the baby.

"I'm probably going to have to."

"That's sticky," Luke said. "And it sounds expensive."

"I'm not worried about money," Max said with a laugh, but as he said the words his facial expression changed rapidly as if he had just thought of something, and Caro realized they were headlong into yet another of those awkward moments. This one about money. She remembered her sister Sadie's comment that Bethany would inherit the proceeds of her mother's estate, which Max would control as her guardian, and she wondered if Max suddenly recognized that the police officer in the Evans family would have known about the funds from the beginning.

"I make a good salary with the Bureau," Max said, sounding angry, making Caro believe he not only realized Sadie would have told them about the money, but also that the family's suspicious detective had probably assumed he had only taken Bethany for her inheritance money. "And I'm fairly good with finances. So I don't need any extraordinary help raising Bethany. We'll do fine."

"I'm sure you will," Pete called over his shoulder as he again lifted the lid of the grill.

Her father sounded so neutral that there was no way Max could believe her dad had thought any further ahead about Bethany's inheritance than the fact that it existed. More than that, though, Pete Evans's disinterest seemed to confirm that he didn't think Max had taken Bethany for her money. When Caro stole a covert glance at Max, she saw surprise register on his face, then a quiet relief, and Caro suppressed her own sigh of relief.

He was doing it. He was getting over all the hurdles just by answering honestly.

Caro's father pressed a fork into the ribs one more time. "And these are done! Luke, bring that tray over here. Caro, go into the house and get the salads." He paused and glanced around. "And somebody call for Hannah. I'm not waiting a minute to eat these. I'm starved."

As always when Pete Evans talked, the family scampered into action. Caro went into the house, Luke took the tray to his father and Lily slid Bethany into the high chair she had set up beside the picnic table.

"She's already eaten," Max said as Lily straightened away.

"Then I have a nice surprise for her." Lily reached across the table and lifted the lid of a serving dish to reveal a thick blueberry bagel. "At the day care we sometimes use these for teething. We have to be careful and watch that the baby doesn't actually break any off, but bagels are sturdy enough and tasty enough to keep a teething child entertained for at least fifteen minutes."

"Oh," Max said, laughing lightly at her ingenuity. "That's great."

"It's Sadie's idea…Sadie Senior," Pete said, setting the plate containing the steaming ribs on the table.

"How is your sister?" Max asked as he took a seat at the picnic table. Caro returned with baked beans. Behind her, her baby sister, Hannah, carried a clear glass bowl of pasta salad.

"The doctors found a mass. They think it's a tumor," Pete said, and Max's breath caught.

"I'm so sorry."

"It's operable," Lily said as both Caro and Hannah slid onto the bench seats of the table and the family began to pass the food. "And we're very optimistic," she added confidently, subtly indicating to Max that they hoped to stay that way. He nodded slightly to show her he understood, and she smiled.

But he noticed that Hannah Evans didn't say anything through the course of lunch. Not even hello. She hardly glanced at Bethany, though Lily and Pete fawned over the baby. When the meal was finished, and Lily insisted the girls do the dishes since the boys, Pete and Luke, had cooked, Luke offered Max a beer and a chair under a shade tree.

Max shook his head. "I need to get Bethany home for a nap."

"Oh, she can nap here," Pete said. "There's a ball game on this afternoon. We can watch the game while the women watch Bethany."

Though the comment didn't seem to penetrate

Caro's concentration as she carried containers of uneaten food to the kitchen, Max saw Hannah stiffen as if offended to be saddled with his child.

"That's okay. I like taking care of Bethany."

He thought it was a good thing to say, a good way to show he wasn't shirking his responsibility, but Hannah stiffened again. Max finally figured out that was because anyone who truly believed he was Brett's father would be upset that he would take responsibility for one child and not another. Especially if he took very good care of the child he acknowledged.

He couldn't win.

"And I really think she needs to be home, in her own crib, for her nap."

Returning from her trip to the kitchen, Caro pushed through the screen door of the back porch. "Then I'll come with you and help. I'll monitor your performance and we'll do a review for your single-dad file."

Max glanced at his feet, then looked up at Caro. "I don't think so. Not today. We're fine," he said, and pulled Bethany from the high chair. Right on cue she rubbed her eyes, then rubbed her face against the soft material of the T-shirt on Max's shoulder. "We need to go home."

Though Caro wanted to shake her little sister silly, she didn't. Not only had Max made real progress with her parents, but also it wasn't realistic to think that he wouldn't have *any* problems blending in. Her sister refusing to talk was a clear statement of mistrust, but it was a civil statement. One that Max and everybody could handle. And one Caro was sure Max would face again. So Hannah had actually been good practice.

All in all, Caro thought the afternoon had gone very well. But she still had to keep herself and Max in contact without being obvious, and she didn't believe she would get beyond his front door if she went to his home. Plus, she couldn't let him retreat into his grandfather's house and never come out, or he wouldn't see that the community was beginning to accept him. But she wasn't worried. There was an easy way she could spend time with him and also keep him in the community. All she had to do was get him to attend the single-dad class he'd enrolled in already.

That was why she called him the next morning. "I notice you haven't attended the single-dad class you signed up for."

"You told me I didn't need it."

"Yes, I did. But you reminded me that because you're an only child, everything you learn in any class is important."

"I'm fine."

"Let's see. You don't want me to come over and give you private lessons. You're refusing to attend classes. It sounds to me like you're cutting out on your deal with Aunt Sadie. You don't want your money back, do you?"

"No. No," he hastily assured her.

"Well, Max, I'm afraid we're going to have to cut you a check for your balance if you don't use our services."

"Caro, you flew to Vegas with me. When we got back, you stayed overnight. You gave me private lessons at my house at least three times. Sadie has earned her money."

"That's not how our bookkeeping works. If you don't use the hours, we'll have to mail you a check to balance our books."

"I won't cash the check."

"Then the money will hang in limbo forever."

"Caro!"

"Come on, Max. The class I want you in starts this morning at ten. Be there."

"But—"

Caro hung up the phone without listening to his protest and hoped his sense of fair play and common courtesy would prevent him from ignoring her invitation.

It did. At ten o'clock that morning Max was in

a new single-dad class, and though the most important member of the group hadn't yet arrived, within ten minutes Max was relaxed and happily part of the session. The men accepted him, as the original single-dad class had, partially because Max was a genuinely nice person and partially because most of the dads were too young to know the Mary Catherine Connor story.

Then Rory Brennan strolled in carrying his three-year-old daughter and Caro breathed an enormous sigh of relief. Not because Rory had finally arrived to take the classes his new young wife was insisting he take even though he wasn't a single dad. But because Caro had deliberately put Max in this class with someone he knew, someone who knew him, someone, like the members of her family, who had been in his clique. Someone who would automatically welcome him.

"Well, for heaven's sake," Rory said as he ambled into the room. "If it isn't the scourge of the football field."

As Caro suspected, Max stiffened, clearly uncomfortable facing a friend after fourteen years of silence and secrets. Still, she had confidence that outspoken Rory would bulldoze through the unpleasantness.

Max quietly said, "Hello, Rory."

"And who is this?" Rory asked, reaching to chuck Bethany on the chin.

Max stiffened again. "This is Bethany," he said quietly.

"She's beautiful."

"Is that your daughter?" Max asked, angling his chin toward the little girl Rory held, slowly picking up the conversation as Caro had hoped he would.

"Yes, this is Amelia." Rory laughed and jiggled the toddler in his arms. "Having a second family is the curse of getting married young, getting divorced when you're still young enough to attract really hot babes and remarrying."

"Yeah, there's a curse," one of the younger dads said with a chuckle. "You hooked up with Tonya Friedman, didn't you?"

"Yes, I did," Rory said proudly, and Caro's stomach did an unexpected flip-flop. She had chosen Rory because he was Max's friend, but she had forgotten that conversation between friends, especially in a class full of men, might not always be "delicate."

"But even though she got pregnant right away," Rory said, "I couldn't marry her until my divorce was final. So I hardly got to know the kid here. That's why my wife says we have trouble communicating."

Everybody except Max laughed heartily and Caro grabbed the opportunity to get them back on the right track. She didn't need Max and Rory to reunite immediately. She just wanted them to meet, begin to get reacquainted and finish later.

"Okay. Since you all seem to know who Rory is, I'll quickly review the disciplining techniques that he missed because he was late. The rest of you pay attention. It doesn't hurt to hear these theories a second time. Then we're going to do some exercises with our toddlers."

"Fine with me. The kid and I can be your demonstration candidates," Rory said, again commandeering center stage.

Caro almost sighed. Not just because she hated the way he referred to his daughter, but because he was an attention stealer. Giving him free rein when he first arrived might have been good for him and Max initially. Unfortunately, he now felt at liberty to speak at will, which was a problem in an intimate class like this.

"Unless old Max over there would like to be the star. You always were star material," Rory continued, plopping down on the floor with his quiet little girl. "You were always the one to get his name in the paper because of your quick hands, and because you were faster than the rest of us." He chuckled. "Of course, now that I think about it, those quick hands and that speed of yours actually got you into trouble, didn't they?''

Hearing Rory's thinly veiled reference to Max getting Mary Catherine Connor pregnant, Caro held back a gasp. She knew Rory was crude. Everybody, except Tonya, seemed to know Rory was crude. But Caro never thought he was vile or that he would publicly talk about something so private.

"Actually, Rory, I'll pick the dad and child who makes the best demonstration team," Caro said, again taking control of the class to stop Rory. "Your daughter looks a little too shy to take the lead and Max's daughter is too young."

"That's right. Your old girlfriend just had her baby. Shame about her being killed—''

"Rory," Caro said, interrupting him. "If you want to discuss this with Max, talk to him after class. We have work to do."

"I'm just saying it's a shame," Rory continued. Because Rory's parents had owned the sewing factory, a car dealership, the convenience store and the dry cleaner, and Rory took over managing them when the senior Brennans retired, he was accustomed to giving orders, not obeying them, and he kept talking as if Caro hadn't spoken. "I heard she never even told you about the baby."

"She didn't," Max said, though he looked loath to respond.

"Well, that's interesting," Rory said, facing Max with a satisfied smile. From the expression on his face, Caro finally saw that Rory was egging Max on. It almost seemed to Caro that he was doing it because he was jealous of Max. Rory, the guy who had everything, was jealous of Max.

Caro could actually see Rory setting up Max to be hated by the class as he said, "You claimed the baby you weren't supposed to know about, but left Mary Catherine twisting in the wind. Why is that? Could it be money? Could that sweet little girl of yours have come into a bundle when her mom was killed?"

Max was about to answer, but, furious, and not about to let Rory get away with this in her class, Caro jumped in. "Rory, this isn't a party where you can stand around and chat. I have two hours to work with you guys to help you with your children. As I told you before, if you want to talk to Max, you do it on your own time."

"Hey, Caro, what the hell is wrong with you?" Rory asked, indignant now. "I'm paying good money to be in this class, too."

"And so are Frank, Al and Jonathan. Now, let's move on."

Caro skillfully shifted the class away from

Rory, who eventually ended up sitting on the last carpet in the back of the room, sulking. Good. She didn't give a damn. Not only was he an idiot, but also he had nearly ruined her plan to prove to Max that people in this town were a lot smarter than to hate him forever without question. She couldn't believe Rory would be so childish, but decided that having money and being the town hotshot had somehow given him the impression that he could do what he wanted when he wanted. But that wouldn't happen in her classroom. When she announced that they were through for the day, Rory left without a word to anyone.

Unfortunately, so did Max.

When Max answered his door that night and saw Caro standing on his front porch, he suspected she had come to apologize for putting him in a class with Rory Brennan. But Max was actually glad she had, because Rory proved his point about his personal relationship with Caro more clearly than Max could ever state it. If Caro continued to be involved with him, even as a friend, she would face the ridicule of the Rory Brennans of this town every day for the rest of her life. Max wasn't about to let that happen any more than he would let Mary Catherine destroy Caro's reputation.

So he sighed and set out to make her mad, to give back her reasons to dislike him, the way he should have weeks ago, before anything got started between them.

"Caro, I know Rory probably filled your head with questions, but I'm not in the mood to talk about Bethany or Brett or anybody tonight. So if you don't mind…"

As he said the last, he began to close the door, but Caro slipped her foot in the opening to prevent him from doing so. "I don't want to leave and I don't want to talk about children, either."

"I don't—"

"Max, I think it's time we talked about us."

Max sighed. "There is no us."

Caro glanced around the darkening neighborhood. "Do you really want to hold this conversation on your front porch where everybody can hear?"

Realizing he was losing this battle, he sighed again. "No."

"Good."

He let her into the foyer and Caro turned and walked right into the living room. Max took a seat on the sofa, leaving the chair for Caro, but rather than take it, Caro sat beside him.

Right beside him. Virtually on his lap. When

she turned to face him, her arm brushed his. Her thigh shifted against his.

''For about a week you've been all but ignoring me.'' She pressed her thigh against his again. ''Now, are you going to try to tell me you don't feel something?''

Max laughed. ''What am I supposed to be feeling?''

''Well,'' Caro said, taking his upper arm and more or less forcing him to look at her. ''What I'm feeling is an incredible need just to be near you, just to hear about your day.''

Sitting so close, staring into her perfect brown eyes, he understood exactly what she was saying—that sexual chemistry was only part of their equation, that he enjoyed talking to her, sharing with her, as much as he wanted to make love to her. Still, he remained neutral. ''Really?''

''Yes. And I'm guessing that's what you feel, too.'' She paused, waited a heartbeat then said, ''Are you going to deny that?''

He remembered his new vow about never lying and realized he was in yet another losing battle. ''No.''

''Okay. What we've just established is that we like each other.''

''Caro, we established that days ago.''

''Weeks ago, actually,'' Caro said, scooting

closer on the sofa, so close now that their thighs didn't brush but were pressed together. ''We also established weeks ago that we're physically attracted to each other. You've kissed me more than once. I would have to be dead not to realize that you want me.''

Max licked his lips. ''Are you building to a point here?''

Caro laughed. ''Yes. The point is, we're one of those couples, Max, who clicked immediately. We both knew it all along. You've already admitted there's something between us. In fact, you warned me that you were going to pursue me. Then something happened that made you change your mind, and suddenly you were fighting it. I know your past and your reputation bother you and I think in your own way you're trying to protect me—''

He began to answer but Caro put a finger over his lips. ''But you're not controlling the game anymore. I am.''

With that she kissed him. Max honest to God thought he felt the earth move, but he realized something else. Something more important. Whatever it was he and Caro felt for each other, it was strong and powerful, but also natural and pure. It was instinct, intuition and wonder all rolled into one. He had known from his first hours with her that she was honest and kind, good and generous. She was the first person in Wilburn to recognize that he was basically a decent man. In Vegas, she had fought to keep her prejudices against him intact. He could see her inward struggles in the expression in her eyes. But in the end she couldn't do it. Just as his attempts to wrestle himself away from her were futile. In only a few weeks, they could read each other, see what others didn't see, and know they were meant to be together.

As her lips softly kissed and caressed his, Max understood what she was saying. They were made for each other. They were a natural combination and it was time to stop fighting.

He shifted her slightly, changed the position of his mouth and took control of the kiss. Instincts and urges buffeted him. The call to make love had never been so intense, or so guileless. He wanted to make love to her because he loved her and he knew she loved him.

And the only thing standing in the way of their being together was Mary Catherine's secret.

No, Max realized, *The only thing standing in their way was the town.* If they didn't live in Wilburn, and had no contact with the residents except to visit for holidays, none of this would matter.

''Come away with me, Caro,'' he whispered

against her mouth, and he felt her lips curve upward in response.

She pulled away slightly. "What?"

Looking into her soft brown eyes, the instincts and urges that pushed at Max suddenly became overwhelming. He took her by the shoulders and held her gaze. "Come away with me."

"To the Casbah?" she asked with a laugh.

"No," Max said urgently, more convinced than ever that this was the right thing to do. "Come with me when I take Bethany home."

She gave him a dumbfounded look. "I can't just leave…"

"I don't think you understood what I said, because I didn't say it well." He paused, drew a quick breath. "Caro, what I'm asking is that you marry me."

Chapter Eight

With Max holding her by the shoulders and staring intently into her eyes, it was hard for Caro to keep a coherent thought. She was shocked that he had asked her to marry him, but even more shocked at how much she wanted to say yes. What he was offering was everything she had ever dreamed of. Life with a good man. A man who would help her raise their children. A man who made her happy. Who made her feel sexy and beautiful. Who made her feel loved. She would follow him to the ends of the earth…if it were possible. But it wasn't. She knew it wasn't.

She licked her suddenly dry lips. "I can't leave," she whispered, her eyes filling with tears. "Max, Aunt Sadie needs me. My parents may be able to handle the day care, but with Aunt Sadie out sick it's my teaching certificate that gives the school credibility. I have to be there every day in some capacity. I can't leave."

"It's okay," Max said, pulling her into his arms to comfort her. "When this house is ready for a real estate agent to put it on the market, I have to go back to Frederick, but we can still see each other on weekends and days off. We'll get married when your Aunt Sadie is better and able to run the day care again." He pushed her away slightly so he could look into her eyes. "I'm not trying to rush you."

Caro licked her lips again. "I don't think you are. But it's not just the day care that keeps me here." She drew a quivering breath, pulled herself out of his arms and rose from the sofa. "Max, all my life I've planned to live in Wilburn with my family. With the exception of my brother Dakota, we've all chosen to live in Wilburn or very close to be with each other, to be part of each other's lives, to support each other. My family is my life. I don't want to give that up."

Max stiffened. "I see."

Caro shook her head. "No. I don't think you do see. I don't just selfishly want this for myself. I want it for my husband, too, and my children. I want you to be a part of the closeness of my family. I saw how happy you were on Sunday. I saw how you fit with my father and brother. Our lives could be very happy here."

Max closed his eyes briefly, then shook his head. "I gave up my rights to this town long ago, and there's no turning back. Just like you can't see yourself leaving, I can't see myself returning."

"But you have returned. You're here now," Caro urgently reminded him. "And things aren't going as badly as you think. People are accepting you. Eventually—"

"Eventually, nothing," Max said, interrupting her. "You saw what happened at the single-dad school with Ray Connor and Rory. There will always be gossip, rumors and innuendo. I won't live that way... I won't ask Bethany to live that way.

"And, Caro, I still have a secret. In Maryland it wouldn't matter. If you didn't know Mary Catherine, I could actually tell you. But you do know Mary Catherine, and we're both connected to this town. Mary Catherine's secret will always be between us."

Caro suddenly realized the odd truth of that. If she didn't know Mary Catherine, if they didn't live in Wilburn, if they had met for the first time six weeks ago, Max's secret would mean nothing.

But because she lived in this town and couldn't know the secret, it would always separate them.

He combed his fingers through his hair. "Look, let's not make this any harder than it has to be. We really like each other. Actually, we love each other. I would also guess we could make each other incredibly happy." He paused long enough to draw a pain-filled breath. "But there are too many things that stand in our way. So rather than drive each other crazy, let's just end this now."

For the second time that night, Max had stunned Caro into silence. She opened her mouth several times to respond, but couldn't think of anything else to say. Her feelings for him were intense and real, but they were new. Her feelings for her family, her feelings about being part of her family and spending her life in this town, were every bit as intense, but they were also time tested. Having Max in her life was recent. Certainly not tested and riddled with problems.

Staring into Max's beautiful blue eyes, she realized this was it. There was no compromise. Worse, for as much as it seemed something had been drawing her to Max all these weeks, she also had to admit that something had been warning her away. This was why. They didn't have a future.

She nodded her agreement with what he had just said, and pivoted away from him, then raced out into the night. She quickly made her way to her parents' house, but instead of going inside, she silently slid through the backyard to the bench swing that hung from the thick branch of one of the oak trees. She collapsed on the padded seat and threw her head back, insisting to herself that she wouldn't feel bad about something that had been doomed from the beginning. But she couldn't help it. She did feel bad. She felt lost, deserted, cheated and hurt. Pain welled up inside her and pushed its way out as tears, and she let them fall.

The next morning, with the darkness replaced by warm July sunlight that streamed in through her bedroom window, Caro lay in her bed, not so much sad as angry. Mostly she was furious with Mary Catherine, because the bottom line was that if Mary Catherine had let Max take responsibility for Brett, none of them would be in this situation right now. She got so mad she bounced out of bed, quickly showered and dressed, then ran out of the house, not even stopping for coffee. She had a nine o'clock single-dad class, but she was sure she would be back by then. If nothing else, she was getting some answers this morning. Max Riley might be an honorable man who wouldn't break the promise he'd made to Mary Catherine, but there was nothing that kept Mary Catherine from talking about herself.

In her blue jeans and bright-red T-shirt, Caro slid through the trees, behind the Connors' garage, and sneaked to the back door. She knocked three times before Mary Catherine finally answered.

"Oh my God! Something happened to Aunt Sadie!"

Realizing Mary Catherine thought the worst because Caro's visit was unexpected, Caro shook her head. "No. I'm sorry. I didn't mean to scare you. Sadie is fine. She's having surgery today, but we're all sure she's going to pull through nicely."

"Oh," Mary Catherine said, obviously a combination of relieved and confused. "So why are you here?"

"I wanted to talk with you."

"And you came to the back door?"

"About Max Riley."

"Oh," Mary Catherine said, glancing around nervously. "I don't think that's a good idea."

"I do. I think it's a wonderful idea. Are you afraid to talk because somebody is here?" Caro asked, peering inside the kitchen, which was empty.

Mary Catherine shook her head. "No, I just don't want to talk to you about Max." Then she caught her breath between her teeth, as if finally realizing something. "He told you!"

"Max told me that you don't want him to have anything to do with Brett. But that's all. He didn't tell me why. He won't explain why he keeps your secret." She shook her head. "You're very lucky, Mary Catherine. He's very loyal to you."

"And I'm as loyal to him as I can be under the circumstances." She put her fingers on Caro's forearm. "You have to understand. I didn't mean for Max to get hurt."

"Well, that part of your plan failed because Max is hurt and he continues to be hurt with every day that passes. Did you know that he's attended three different enrollments of the single-dad school and in two of the sessions somebody harassed him about not taking responsibility for Brett?"

"I'm sorry."

"No, you're not!" Caro said, interrupting her. "Mary Catherine, if you were sorry, this wouldn't be happening! You would change what's going on. You would let Max take responsibility for Brett so that people would stop hating him!"

Mary Catherine licked her lips and Caro's eyes narrowed. "What's wrong with what I just said? Why can't you let Max take responsibility for Brett?"

"Look," Mary Catherine said as she began to close the back door. "I can't talk about this. So just stay out of it!"

Caro put her foot in the door, preventing Mary Catherine from closing it. "You know, I'm not quite the nice guy Max Riley is. He may not be able to expose your secrets, but I never made that promise to you. In fact," she said, catching Mary Catherine's gaze as she played her trump card. "If you're not willing to talk with me, maybe I'll just ask my sisters Maria and Sadie what they remember about the year Brett was conceived. I'm sure if the three of us think about it long enough, we'll figure it out."

Mary Catherine's eyes narrowed and her expression became fierce. "Caro, you don't know who you're playing with here…"

"Maybe you don't know who you're playing with, Mary Catherine," Caro said boldly, though inside she was quaking. She had absolutely nothing to back up her threat except that if Mary Catherine refused to talk to her she would ask around, opening the situation to speculation again. "If you won't tell me the truth, I can find it. But if you force me to go looking on my own, trust me, I'll stir up a nest of trouble. Starting with my own sisters, who are going to wonder why you weren't honest with them." She paused for a second, making sure Mary Catherine understood what she was saying. "You can threaten me all you want, but in the end you're the one who is going to lose friends if you drive me to look elsewhere for answers, because I won't be bound by any promise then."

"Are you saying you'll agree to keep my secret if I tell you?"

"I'm saying that's the only way you'll keep this situation a secret. If you force me to ask around, even if I personally never tell what I find, I'll stir up suspicions."

Mary Catherine motioned for Caro to enter and directed her to the kitchen table. Then she turned and walked to the folding doors that opened the room to the rest of the house, and shut them tightly.

"I want the whole story, Mary Catherine."

Mary Catherine took a seat at the table beside Caro and for a few seconds only stared at her empty coffee cup. Finally she said, "I guess you would." She glanced up at Caro. "I saw Max kiss you at the mall the other day."

Though Caro's first instinct was to cringe in embarrassment, she held Mary Catherine's gaze. "I like him a lot."

"You should. He's a good person."

"Then why won't you let him see Brett, help with Brett, be a part of Brett's life?"

"I won't let Max take an active role in Brett's life because he's not Brett's father."

Caro only gaped at Mary Catherine. "What?"

"Max isn't Brett's father. Rory Brennan is."

If Caro hadn't been sitting, she knew she would have collapsed from the shock of that disclosure. It took several seconds of working to prevent herself from hyperventilating before she could say, "Are you kidding?"

"Nope. Rory Brennan is Brett's father. Right before graduation Max's senior year, he and I had a fight about him leaving Wilburn with his parents. Because I was only a sophomore, I wasn't going anywhere and I didn't want him to leave. I thought he could stay with his grandfather. I even asked his grandfather about it, and his grandfather was more than happy to let Max have a room at his house. Max could have gone to Pitt as easily as he went to Florida State. But Max wanted to go. He had his life all mapped out and it seemed like it didn't include me. He insisted that it did. And that once he had his degree and was on the road to having a career and therefore an income, we would get married."

"But you didn't believe him?"

Mary Catherine shrugged. "I was sixteen. Four

years was like a lifetime. I couldn't see him coming back for me."

"So you slept with one of his best friends?"

"Essentially," Mary Catherine said with a sigh as she toyed with the salt and pepper shakers on the table and wouldn't meet Caro's gaze. "I hadn't intended to sleep with Rory, just go out with him to make Max see that if he left, our relationship was at risk, but Rory was... persuasive."

Caro's eyes narrowed in fury. "He raped you?"

Mary Catherine shook her head. "No."

"So why not make Rory take responsibility for Brett?"

Mary Catherine sighed heavily. "Caro, I'm going to tell you this whole story because I really don't want you asking around. But that means you have to keep it completely confidential."

Though she wasn't sure it was the right thing to do, Caro nodded.

"Okay," Mary Catherine said. "The fourth time we went out, Rory needed to do some 'business' with 'friends.' It was something that had to do with his parents' car dealership. I'm guessing Rory had somebody who got him stolen parts or stolen cars or something. I didn't want to know and no one really explained. I just thought it was so cool, you know, so grown-up to be going to a garage at midnight and making a clandestine deal. So much better than going to college. And I insisted I get to go along. But the deal went sour. The guy who was supposed to bring something for Rory didn't have it.''

She paused and poured herself a cup of coffee from a white carafe on the table. Caro didn't say a word.

Finally, after adding cream to her coffee and staring at the murky liquid for several seconds, Mary Catherine continued. ''I didn't get the details. The only part of the thing I really understood was that Rory beat the hell out of the guy who didn't come through for him.''

''Oh.''

''He almost killed him. I'm convinced his intent was to kill him. But one of the other guys with us stopped him.''

''So when you realized you were pregnant you were afraid to tell Rory because you thought he would hurt you?''

Mary Catherine laughed slightly and shook her head. ''Rory has always been jealous of Max, so I think he would have been thrilled to have gotten Max's girlfriend pregnant. I think he would have paraded me like a trophy.''

''And you didn't want that?''

"No, what I didn't want was to have my child connected to Rory for the rest of his life. Worse, I didn't want Rory having visitation rights because I was scared for Brett. I still am scared for Brett. Having Rory take full responsibility for Brett and become his father is my worst nightmare."

"I see," Caro said, because she did. The fact that Tonya Friedman insisted Rory go to single-dad classes had sent up a red flag for Caro from the beginning, particularly since Rory had children from his first marriage and should know how to care for a toddler. But she thought Rory was simply a bad dad because he was self-absorbed. If Mary Catherine's instincts were right, if Rory had a temper severe enough to almost kill somebody, Tonya sending him to single-dad school was like putting a bandage on a broken leg.

Caro suddenly feared for the adorable little girl Rory brought with him to class.

"Because I was so afraid of Rory," Mary Catherine said, breaking the uncomfortable silence, "Max agreed to let me pretend he was the father of my baby. At the time, with Max's family planning to move away, Max and I thought it was a good idea. It was supposed to be easy. Not a big deal. And in a way it has been perfect."

"For you."

Mary Catherine nodded. "Yes. For me. It has protected both me and Brett from Rory."

"It hasn't been easy for Max."

"I know."

"You could fix this just by saying that Max isn't Brett's father. You don't have to say Rory is Brett's dad. Just say Max isn't. That would get Max off the hook and still keep your secret."

She shook her head. "Not really. Rory would figure out that if Max isn't the father then he is."

"It's been fourteen years, maybe he wouldn't make the connection."

"He would make the connection eventually. And then he would be in Brett's life."

Caro stared at the print tablecloth in front of her. She understood Mary Catherine's fear. Maybe she understood it too well. Because Caro had come from a close, loving family, as Mary Catherine had, she knew that getting involved with someone like Rory wouldn't merely be frightening, it would be intolerable. "I don't know what to say."

"Say you'll keep the secret."

"I already made that promise," Caro said, realizing that because she had she was now in the same predicament Max was.

Mary Catherine peered up from her coffee.

"What I told you obviously didn't help you figure out what to do with Max."

"No, it didn't," Caro answered honestly. "There is more about this situation with me and Max than simply the issue of Brett."

Mary Catherine brightened. "Oh," she said, sounding relieved. "That's good... I mean that's not good, but you know, it's just better if he stays away from Wilburn."

Not sure if she should be angry with Mary Catherine or feel sorry for her because she was as trapped as Max was, Caro rose from her seat.

Mary Catherine grabbed her hand to keep her from leaving. "The only time it's really hard is when Max is home. I like that he stays away."

Caro drew a long breath. That, apparently, was another good thing Max was doing. Staying away to help Mary Catherine preserve her sanity. She almost couldn't believe what a mess one lie had made, and clearly Mary Catherine felt the trouble was worth it.

"I have to get to class now," Caro said, edging out of the Connors' kitchen.

Mary Catherine nodded and Caro sneaked out of the house the same way she had come in. Technically, she was no closer to solving her problem with Max than she was before she knocked on Mary Catherine's kitchen door. But something even more important had come from the meeting. With the realization that Brett wasn't the only child in this situation, Caro also knew that she had to protect Rory's daughter. If there was an answer, she had to find it.

And quickly.

"There's a hole in your plan with Mary Catherine," Caro said when Max answered her knock that night.

"I don't have a plan with Mary Catherine."

"Sure you do," she said, stepping into the foyer. "You agreed to help her keep Brett away from his real father by never disclaiming that Mary Catherine's baby was yours."

Max sucked in his breath.

"I'm not that smart or psychic. I went to see Mary Catherine this morning."

"And she told you?" Max asked, obviously stunned that Mary Catherine had revealed her secret.

"I threatened to start asking around and made her realize my sisters would be the people who would eventually figure out the truth, if forced to really think about it."

Max grimaced. "I hadn't thought of that."

"You and Mary Catherine didn't think about a lot of things," Caro said. "For one, there's more of a problem here than just your reputation and Brett's safety."

"I don't follow."

"Max, talking to Mary Catherine, it didn't take me long to realize that Rory's quiet little girl and his wife's insistence that he attend single-dad school, even though he's not a single dad or a first-time father, are probably confirmation that what Mary Catherine suspected was true. This is a man who can't control his temper. He probably lashes out at his wife and kids. Mary Catherine was lucky to have seen the worst of him on that date because technically that kept her from telling him about Brett. And," Caro admitted softly, "I think she had every reason to be afraid."

Clearly relieved that she agreed, Max nodded. "So did I."

"Okay. We all agree on that. This secret needs to be kept because Brett needs to be protected from Rory…"

This time Max shook his head. "Though I think Brett needs to be protected from Rory, I no longer agree with what Mary Catherine is doing. Brett is thirteen. He has a right to know who his real father is. I do agree that Rory shouldn't get visitation rights with Brett without supervision, but I no longer agree that Brett should grow up not knowing his roots."

Caro stared at him. "I can't believe you feel that way!"

"And I can't believe you don't understand what I'm saying. None of us picks our families. True, some of us are luckier than others. But Brett has a perfectly good set of grandparents who don't even know he exists. Rory's parents are wonderful people and the past few years haven't been kind to them. I did some investigating myself today and I discovered that the Brennans lost the dry-cleaning business to competition, their sewing factory closed, and their car dealership was sold for peanuts. The only thing they had left was the little convenience store on Main Street and I heard Rory is planning to sell to Lacy Vickroy. So now they have nothing. Wouldn't it be nice for them to discover they have a grandchild they didn't know about?"

"They have plenty of grandchildren."

"But they still have a right to know Brett!" Max sighed. "What I'm trying to say is that there are more people affected here than just me, Mary Catherine, Brett and Rory. And it's time, Caro."

"Then you are really going to hate my idea."

He drew a long breath. "Probably, but let's hear it."

"Mary Catherine told me that your coming back to town is what raised all the questions again. She also feels that you stay away to protect her secret.''

"That's part of it."

"So I thought that if you would claim Brett, act like a father to him, there would be no reason for Rory to ever get suspicious and discover he's Brett's dad, and it would also make it possible for you to remain in Wilburn.''

Max shook his head. "I can't do it."

"But think about it, Max. The hole in Mary Catherine's plan is that people who know you know you wouldn't desert a child. If you take responsibility for Brett, the hole closes. And it solves all our problems. Brett gets a dad, Mary Catherine's secret stays safe, you can live in Wilburn and then you and I can look for a way to protect Rory's other kids.''

"If I were only trying to find a way to be with you, yes, I would think it was a fine plan. I love you. I would love to be with you. But it's not fair to Brett. It's not fair to Rory's parents who have suffered enough in the past years, watching Rory destroy their businesses and throw them on the brink of bankruptcy. It's also not fair for me to be accused of doing something that I didn't do.''

Realizing he was right, and that her solution was almost as much of a bandage as Tonya Friedman's sending Rory to single-dad school, Caro squeezed her eyes shut. "I'm sorry."

"Caro, there is no reason to be sorry. What you're doing is what I have been doing for the past several years, looking for the answer to a nearly impossible question. When I never discovered that answer, the only thing I could do was keep my promise."

"I just want us to be together."

Max pulled her into his arms. "I want us to be together, too."

He kissed her and though Caro knew it had only been his intention to comfort her, the kiss quickly became hungry and passionate. She couldn't decide if the shift had been his design or hers. She only knew that one second he was kissing her softly and the next his mouth slanted over hers hungrily. He crushed her against him, greedily devouring her mouth, and Caro reveled in the feelings and instincts that sprang up inside her as she twined her arms around his neck and edged even closer. She wanted to make love to him. She wanted to feel the length of his body pressed against hers. She wanted to take him inside her. She wanted to be his.

This was Max. The man she loved. Every other man she had dated or thought she loved faded into a distant memory. Good and decent, strong and sexy, smart and wonderful Max Riley loved her. And she loved him.

But as quickly as he had begun kissing her, Max backed away. His hands slowly slid from her shoulders and he took a step back. "Nothing has really changed, Caro."

She licked her lips, tasting him, wanting him, yet knowing what he said was true. Nothing had changed. And there didn't seem to be any more options for finding a way to make things change.

When she didn't say anything, Max took another step back, positioning himself completely out of her reach. "You better leave."

He was right. She knew he was right, but leaving was the last thing she wanted to do and that confused her. Usually, when something about her life was as clear as this, Caro had no trouble pulling herself away. This time, however, even in the midst of an unsolvable problem, she wanted to stay.

She gave him a weak smile. "I thought that if I found a way for you to live in Wilburn…"

"I understand, but, Caro, this isn't just about Brett and my tarnished reputation. The truth is, I'm not sure I would ever really want to live in this town again."

"Because of the way they hurt and mistrusted you?"

"That's part of it," Max said, taking a seat on the bottom step of the foyer stairway. He patted the spot beside him and Caro sat, too. "Haven't you ever wondered why I didn't have a hard time staying away?"

She nodded. "Yeah."

"Even though everybody knew me to be a fairly decent person, I easily got the blame for something Rory did."

"But you *took* the blame."

"Not really. I just never denied paternity. I never said Brett was mine. Yet everybody assumed he was."

"You were dating Mary Catherine."

"We broke up and Mary Catherine had several public dates with Rory. But I was the one accused. No one ever pointed the finger in his direction."

Realizing the truth of what Max said, Caro frowned. "Why do you think that is?"

"No one wanted to. It was much easier to gossip about me than to gossip about the son of the people who owned the sewing factory that employed most of the townspeople." He paused and sighed heavily. "You insinuated in Las Vegas that it was unfair for me to get away with a bunch of high-school pranks because I was a star football player. So I know you agree with me. You hate the favoritism as much as I do.''

"But it's like that in every small town."

"Yeah, maybe. And people who have money might also get away with a lot of things in the big city, but at least in a bigger city a falsely accused person isn't known by everybody he or she meets on the street. At least in a city there's a larger pool from which to draw friends, people who will believe you, side with you, maybe even defend you."

Caro frowned. "I suppose."

"Caro, I know. No one—not one person—in this town gave me the benefit of the doubt. If I had stayed here the biggest part of my life would have been spent dodging a lie. And even if we somehow fix this, I won't raise Bethany or any other child in a town that was so quick to accuse me and so quick to forgive Rory."

He paused, caught Caro's chin between his thumb and forefinger and said, "I love you. I want to make love to you so much I can taste it. But I can't live here. If you want to move to Maryland with me, I would marry you tomorrow. The choice is yours."

Chapter Nine

When Max showed up for single-dad class the next morning, Caro didn't think it was because he had changed his mind about living in Wilburn. He hadn't even kissed her goodbye the night before, and was determined to stand by his decision that if she wouldn't move away with him, they had to part. She didn't believe one night's sleep had worked a miracle. Though she was glad he at least wanted to see her enough that he came to school.

She also recognized that the real reason Max had such a low opinion of their hometown was that he had been away from Wilburn for too long. He had been burned by the residents of her community, and because he had little to no interaction with them, he didn't realize most weren't so cowardly that they wouldn't stand up to Rory in a real crisis.

And as far as Caro was concerned this was a crisis. Now that she was alerted to the possibility that he could be hurting his children, there was no way in hell she was letting him get away with it. She also expected that if she found sufficient evidence to go to the authorities, they wouldn't let Rory's money or his position stop them from doing their duty.

The funny part of it was, if she carefully monitored the daughter he brought to the single-dad school, found something and reported it, she would not only protect Amelia, she would also provide proof that Mary Catherine could take to court to keep Rory away from Brett. Mary Catherine would finally tell the truth, Brett could finally meet his extended family and Max could begin the healing process he needed over the town's false accusations.

She was sure that once everything came out in the open and people saw the truth, many would apologize and Max would see that they weren't as bad as he had thought. All she needed was time to make this work, and as long as Max kept coming to single-dad class she had that time.

If it weren't for the fact that she would have to

find signs of abuse on sweet Amelia, Caro would consider this a perfect plan.

"Hi, Max. Bethany," Caro said, greeting Max and his daughter when they walked into the play-room. She immediately reached for Bethany. Max handed her to Caro and then stripped off his back-pack-type diaper bag and rotated his shoulders as if it was a great relief.

"I didn't expect to see you here today," she said, making conversation. She couldn't tell him about her plan to look for signs of abuse because the other two single dads were already in the room, and even if she and Max were alone, that information would be confidential. Still, she did intend to keep the lines of honest communication open between her and Max.

Busy with his diaper bag, Max said, "I actually hadn't intended to come. But I remembered that I had left a few of Bethany's things here and I figured I might as well get in one last lesson be-fore I'm forced to be on my own."

"Oh." The resoluteness and finality in his voice surprised Caro. She hadn't expected him to have completely changed his opinion from the night before, but she had thought his coming to school at least meant he wanted to see her. Meet-ing for class was a very good way to keep seeing each other without promises or unrealistic expectations until she found a way to do something about Rory. If Max quit coming, they might drift apart. Worse, Max could finish his grandfather's house and leave, and Caro would never know.

Unfortunately, before she could say anything, Rory Brennan walked into the single-dad class, toting Amelia.

Given Max's solemn mood, Caro almost changed the plan she had made to get Amelia alone. She knew Max wasn't going to like this, but she also knew in the end he would understand. She set Bethany in an available play yard and walked over to Rory with a smile. She reached for Amelia. "Let me take her," she said to Rory. "I'm giving you guys a fifteen- or twenty-minute gab session. This is where you all just go outside and talk about the problems you're having raising your kids. Maybe share information. I'll call you when it's time to come back in, and in the meantime I'll entertain the kids."

Max gaped at Caro, but Rory rubbed his hands together with glee. "Thank God! I don't know what in the hell Tonya hopes to accomplish by forcing me and Amelia together, but it's starting to wear on my nerves."

Which was exactly what Caro was afraid of. "Well, I'll take care of Amelia for the next few

minutes. You guys go sit on the picnic tables in
the yard. Take a break.''

Though Max looked equal parts confused and
angry, he did as Caro asked. He delayed the trip
by filling a paper cup from the stash by the watercooler, and even backhandedly wasted more
time when he gave Rory and the other two fathers
the idea to take a glass of water with them, too.
But eventually all four dads left.

When they were gone, Caro led the three toddlers, including Amelia, to the center of the room.
She set three clean carpets on the floor and directed the kids to sit on the rectangle she created.
When they were settled, she went to the play yard
and extracted Bethany to bring her into the game,
too.

Careful to structure the playtime so that it was
exactly that, playtime, because she didn't want to
be accused of making an illegal search, Caro
couldn't do anything overt. But she examined
every exposed inch when Amelia's little blue
jeans rose as a result of a stretch. She looked for
marks or bruises when the little girl reached for a
toy. She even got the opportunity to look more
closely when Amelia asked to use the potty. But
with equal parts relief and disappointment, Caro
found nothing.

Still, though there were no signs of abuse on

Amelia, Caro had no intention of stopping her pursuit to discover if Rory Brennan hurt his children. But she knew she couldn't do anything haphazardly. She had to be careful.

Recognizing she had done all she could do today, she called the men back into the playroom, held a quick class and dismissed everyone as if nothing were amiss.

The second Rory was out the door, Max turned to her, Bethany on his arm. "What the hell was that all about?"

"Nothing."

"I don't believe that."

"Max," Caro said, trying to sound innocent and casual, "you and Rory had a problem in the last class. That few minutes alone was my way of giving you the chance to find neutral ground." She paused, then said, "Did you find it?"

"Not really."

Not surprised, Caro began gathering toys from the carpeted floor. "You will."

"I sincerely doubt it and you know why."

Realizing that had been the stupidest excuse she could have chosen, Caro shrugged and decided that rather than try to make something stupid look sane, she would say nothing more on that subject.

Max also said nothing, just hung around nervously by the watercooler. Bethany's diaper bag bounced off the corresponding trash can as he let it hang loosely by his leg. He had everything he needed to go, but wasn't going.

Caro continued to gather toys. She suspected that he didn't want to leave her any more than she wanted him to leave, but she couldn't think of a reason to hold him at the day care. Particularly not when she had another class in a few minutes. Then inspiration struck.

"Hey, why don't I come over for dinner?" she said, still gathering toys, and actually looking away from him so her invitation would sound off-hand and ordinary, giving them a way to go back to where they were before he asked her to marry him. A way to pretend the discussion from the day before hadn't happened.

When she rose, she saw Max swallow hard and take a small step backward, away from her. "I already told you how I feel about us seeing each other. I'm not changing my mind." Holding Bethany on his arm, he continued to back away from her. "Look, I've got to go."

"Okay," Caro said, upset that he had refused her but not devastated, because she had her plan to work this out. Once she resolved the mess with Rory, things would be fine. "Bye," she said, waving slightly to Bethany.

"Bye, Caro," Max whispered, as if he was saying goodbye forever and for good, then he swung around and virtually ran out of the building.

The way he said goodbye sent a shaft of fear through her because again what he said had an awful ring of finality to it. But she took a long breath and told herself to stop worrying. Even if he did feel they needed to part, she had a plan that would bring them back together.

At six-thirty that night, when the last child at the day care was being carted off by an exhausted-looking mother, Caro realized that her parents hadn't put in as much as a token appearance all day. She and Hannah had been covering for them because they had driven to Pittsburgh the day before to be with Sadie through the surgery to remove her tumor. But Caro had seen their car pull in to the garage in the early afternoon. She took that to mean Sadie's surgery went well, and they had returned to pick up their day-care duties as they had promised. Now she wasn't so sure.

She locked the day-care door, walked home and stepped into the kitchen to find her mother and father at the table. Hannah leaned against the sink, Luke straddled a chair and Sadie Junior dumbfoundedly rested against the refrigerator.

"What's up?" Caro asked, her heart leaping to her throat when she saw the horrible expressions on the faces around her.

"The surgery didn't go as well as expected. Aunt Sadie's going to have to have both chemotherapy and radiation treatments."

Fully understanding Sadie Junior's dumbfounded look, Caro fell to an empty chair by the table. "Oh, God."

"The prognosis isn't necessarily bad," her father began, but he choked up and had to stop.

Luke took over for him. "But the treatments are difficult. She's going to be sick for a while." He drew a long breath. "Caro, will you be able to keep up the single-dad school?"

"Of course, I can do this until school starts."

"We need you to commit all through the winter."

"The chemo takes six months," Caro's mother said. "Which means we need you and Hannah to do everything your Aunt Sadie had done at the day care. Plus, you'll still have to be available every weekend, probably most weekends for single-dad emergencies."

"That's no problem," Caro quickly assured them. "I'll take a sabbatical from school."

Luke squeezed her hand. "Okay. That's good.

We're set. We've got somebody to cover everything.''

"Yeah, we do,'' Caro agreed, knowing that this solidified her need to stay in Wilburn and would even illustrate to Max how important family was. In fact, she desperately wanted to talk to him. She wanted his comfort, but she also wanted him to realize she really couldn't leave.

Though she stayed with her family throughout their nearly silent dinner, Caro excused herself after the dishes were washed and raced to Max's grandfather's house to talk to Max.

Unfortunately, when she turned the corner that took her to Max's street, she saw Max standing in the driveway with his parents. Though his SUV was always stuffed with Bethany's things, this time the vehicle was packed to capacity. His mom and dad stood beside the open door, and Max was clearly poised to get in behind the steering wheel. As she walked up the driveway she could see Bethany was fastened in her safety seat.

"Hi,'' she said, and though she had intended for the greeting to be casual, in one syllable she managed to sound both bewildered and angry.

"Caro,'' Max said, spinning to face her.

"Yeah. It's me. Obviously, you weren't expecting me.''

She didn't want to sound like a scorned lover.

She hated the fact that she sounded wounded and confused. But she was wounded and confused. Max didn't have to get a chalkboard and write it out for her. He was leaving town, and he had no intention of telling her.

"Hi, Mr. and Mrs. Riley," she said, extending her hand to shake theirs. "I'm Caro Evans, I've been Max and Bethany's teacher at the single-dad school."

"The single-dad school!" Mrs. Riley said with a laugh. Tall and regal, with dark hair and dark, penetrating eyes, Mia Riley was still a beautiful woman. "What a wonderful idea!"

"Max didn't tell you about his lessons?" Caro said, feeling as if someone had stabbed her in the heart. All this time she thought she and Max were contemplating a permanent relationship and Max hadn't even told his parents about her. Not even that she was his teacher.

"No, he didn't. Though he should have because it would have put our minds at ease about him and Bethany," Max's dad said, shaking his head. "We should have had some kind of dad school in my day," he added. "Would have made my life a lot easier."

"So what's going on?" Caro said, facing Max and forcing the issue because she wasn't just hurt or mad, she felt betrayed. And if she was being betrayed, she wanted to know.

"My parents are going to finish preparing the house for sale."

"Oh," she said, realizing that this hadn't been a spur-of-the-moment decision. People who lived in Florida would need at least a day of nonstop driving to be in Pennsylvania. "So you would have known this last night. Maybe even the day before..."

"Caro," Max said, reaching to clasp her forearms.

She shook off his hands. "No. Get away from me. And stay away from me," she said, and pivoted to bolt down the sidewalk.

"Caro!"

She heard Max calling her but all she could think about was what an idiot she was. He had told her over and over again that he didn't want to be a part of her life. Yet she kept trying to fix things. His decision to leave town, before his work on the house was done and without saying goodbye, only proved what he had been saying all along. He didn't want to fix this. He didn't want her enough to even try.

She felt like a fool.

"Caro..."

"Forget it, Max! I just came by to tell you that

because of Aunt Sadie's treatment, I'll be taking over the day care completely for at least six months. But it seems you didn't need any further explanation about why I couldn't leave with you. So, go. I'm fine. Everything's fine.''

With that she turned and ran away. Tears filled her eyes, but she resolutely refused to let them fall. Damn him. She wasn't crying over a man who didn't even want her enough to try!

Pain sliced at Max as he watched Caro go. It was everything he could do to keep from running after her. Not just because she was clearly hurt that he hadn't told her his plan to leave town, but also because he wanted her. He could not believe he couldn't have her. He could not believe that their circumstances wouldn't budge and couldn't be budged enough that they could have a life together. But the truth was, he couldn't live in a town full of gossip and lies and she couldn't leave. Her family needed her. He couldn't keep her from fulfilling her responsibilities. It was better for her to hate him because then she wouldn't waste time pining for him the way he knew he would pine for her.

So he watched her go. Pain gripped his heart. He knew he would never find another woman he could love the way he loved Caro, and the future stretched before him dark and empty.

Chapter Ten

Two days later, Max stood in front of the door to Sadie Junior's apartment in Pittsburgh. He hesitated a second, then knocked. When she answered, her blunt-cut black hair swinging as she pulled open the door, she looked at him as if he were crazy.

"What do you want?" she asked, her gruff tone confirming what he suspected. She would rather shoot him than talk to him and that made him crazy for knocking on her door.

He handed her the plastic bag containing the cup he had retrieved from the wastebasket of the single-dad school.

"Here. This is all yours."

"Well, gee thanks. And it's not even my birthday or anything."

Max couldn't help it, he laughed. "Still the same old Sadie."

"Still the same old Max. I understand my sister's been crying since the day you left. I should punch you. But I think we both grew out of that. Now what I'm planning is a lot more sinister…"

"Sadie, save it for somebody who cares." He nodded in the direction of the plastic bag he had just handed her. "That cup has Rory Brennan's fingerprints and DNA on it. What I'm going to tell you I'm only revealing because I expect the confidentiality any informant would get from you as a detective until you crack this case. And I'm going to trust you'll honor that," he said, but didn't give Sadie a chance to confirm she would uphold the bargain. "Mary Catherine Connor witnessed a transaction between Rory Brennan and some people I'm guessing provided stolen auto parts for Rory fourteen years ago. The deal went sour and Rory beat the hell out of the guy who cheated him, so when Mary Catherine discovered she was pregnant with his child she was terrified."

Sadie gaped at him. "Damn it," she muttered, combing her fingers through her hair to force it off her face. "Rory Brennan is Brett's father?"

"What? Sorry that you don't get to hate me anymore?"

Sadie drew a slow, controlled breath, then looked Max in the eye. "Finish your story."

"All this happened fourteen years ago, but leopards don't change their spots. I just spent some time in Wilburn. Mostly I kept to myself, but I couldn't help noticing that the sewing factory is closed, the car dealership has been sold, and the dry cleaner went out of business. Yet, Rory still seems to have a heck of a lot of clout..."

"Old habits die hard for people in a small town."

"He also seems to have a great deal of money."

Sadie shook her head. "He could be spending the proceeds of the sale of any of the three businesses..."

"The dry cleaner went out of business and the factory closed. Neither building is in use. I checked the records at the courthouse and discovered neither building was sold...neither *company* was sold. The car dealership went for peanuts. Not enough money to support Rory, his kids, two wives and his parents."

"And you think Rory's involved in something illegal."

"I would bet a year's salary."

"Hmm. That's something, since I heard people

in the FBI make big bucks. At least bigger bucks than I make.'' She paused and caught Max's gaze. ''Why aren't *you* investigating?''

He laughed. ''Are you kidding? Not only have I been taking the rap for Rory getting Mary Catherine pregnant, but he and I had a disagreement at the single-dad school. If I investigate, or take this to the Bureau, it will look like nothing but revenge or sour grapes. Plus, you're in western Pennsylvania. Off the top of your head you can probably tell me about three garages being investigated as possible chop shops. And if those two reasons aren't enough, you can slip into Wilburn virtually unnoticed to investigate. I can't.''

Sadie sighed. ''All of that makes sense. But, Max, you've got to know that even with my background knowledge, this is still a long shot.''

''I know.''

''And proving Rory's a criminal doesn't help the fact that he's Brett's father. It's not going to change anything for you unless you tell people he's Brett's father, and since you've never done it before, I'm guessing you can't.''

''No, I can't,'' Max agreed. ''But if you can get Rory out of the way by getting him arrested, one of us could convince Mary Catherine to go to Rory's parents and tell them about Brett. I agree with her wanting to keep Brett away from

Rory. But Rory's parents don't deserve to be punished, and Brett has a right to know about his other family.''

Sadie nodded. ''I agree.''

''So, you'll do it?''

She nodded again. ''Yeah.'' She cleared her throat. ''Look, Max, I don't know how to say this, but I feel like fourteen years' worth of hell.''

''You don't have to feel like hell. When this all went down I was eighteen and Mary Catherine was sixteen. At the time, making everybody believe I was Brett's father seemed like a logical thing to do. Neither one of us wanted anybody to feel bad. We did what we thought we had to do.''

Max turned to leave, but Sadie caught his arm. ''If I straighten this out... If I connect him to a crime and he goes to jail, does this mean you're coming back to Wilburn?''

''No.''

Sadie gaped at him. ''You're not doing this so you can marry my sister?''

''I would love to marry your sister. But I won't live in a town that never gave me the benefit of the doubt and harbors criminals. It's obvious from the amount that Rory's spending that he must be making his money through something illegal, but everybody turns a blind eye. More than that, though, both Caro and I suspect that Rory is abusing his children. Yet I don't see anybody but Caro trying to prove that... And that reminds me, before Caro gets herself in over her head, you might want to investigate in that direction, too. Rory has a three-year-old named Amelia. I didn't see any clear sign he was abusing her but he has a wicked temper and somebody needs to check into that.''

With that he walked away and Sadie stared after him, holding what she considered to be the evidence that Max Riley really did love her sister, and furious with herself for missing more than one thing that had been right under her nose for the past several years.

For the next few weeks, Caro was run ragged at the day care. As the director of the facility, making assignments and day plans, running the single-dad school and also filling in for her parents who were spending most of their time in Pittsburgh where her Aunt Sadie had begun her chemotherapy, she didn't have ten minutes to herself.

But at night, right before she fell asleep, she would think about Max. The first night she was so hurt and so angry she cried in fits and starts. But the whole next week, she cried every minute she wasn't working. The week after that she felt better, and only cried every other night. Now, this week, she finally felt she was regaining some of her strength, and she thought, maybe, just maybe, she would live.

Actually, she had to live because Sadie Senior wasn't coming back for a long time. At least six months. With her doctor in Pittsburgh, the family had decided it would be best for Aunt Sadie to live near the hospital with one of her sisters. That wasn't merely to save Sadie the effort of a two-hour drive to her treatments. It was also because Caro's Aunt Martie had two sons whom Sadie didn't often see. Liam and Leland, an attorney and an architect, were bright, devilish practical jokers and Sadie had always adored them. Spending six months in the company of two nephews who would make her laugh was exactly what Sadie needed.

It was probably what Caro needed, too. Six months with somebody who would make her laugh. But she wasn't going to get it because she was the head of the day care now. She made the schedules, taught the classes, participated in the day-to-day activities. So serious was her family that one specific person needed to be in charge to ensure continuity of services, that Caro arranged for a sabbatical from her teaching job.

And now here she was, Caro thought as she looked around the simple rooms filled with early-

morning sun. She was Sadie Senior. She was a
woman with a broken heart, vowing never to love
again, and satisfying her maternal instincts by caring for other people's children. She'd always
thought caring for oodles of children was her des-
tiny. But until she met Max it had been a wonderful choice. *Her* choice. Today she only felt like
an old maid. Or a discarded shoe.

She considered that and decided the shoe anal-
ogy fit better. She was a discarded shoe. Probably
a loafer. Something dependable and simple that
everybody used until it fell apart.

"Stop that," Caro scolded herself as she bent
to retrieve a fallen toy, disgusted that she was still
upset by Max Riley's betrayal. But she was. She
really was. The man had her completely fooled.
Even now she found herself wishing he would
just appear at the day-care door, wishing she
could see him, wishing to hear his voice…

"So, when do classes start?"

When Max's voice echoed through the empty
playroom, Caro went perfectly still. At first, she
wondered if she hadn't conjured him up out of
sheer longing, and she stayed bent over the toy,
taking deep breaths, praying she wasn't
hallucinating.

"I want to be permanently enrolled."

Caro straightened and swung around to face

him, unwilling to fall for his lines anymore. He told her he loved her and wanted to marry her, then didn't even have the decency to tell her he was leaving town. "Get out."

Max walked in anyway. "I think there's still time left on my bill. I want it."

"I'll send you the money."

"Sadie needs the money."

"I'll reimburse her out of my own savings account."

Max sighed. "Caro, I don't have a whole heck of a lot of time here, so let's save the argument for later. I need for you to shut up and listen."

"I don't want to shut up and listen. My God, I gave you the benefit of the doubt about everything and in the end you deserted me."

Max grabbed her upper arms, hauled her against him and kissed her. He pressed his mouth against hers until her shock wore off and her lips slackened beneath his, then he deepened the kiss. His hands slid from her arms to her back, and he held her so tightly Caro didn't think he would ever let her go.

When he pulled away, he said, "I didn't want to desert you."

Though her heart was beating a million beats a second, her head was spinning, and she wanted nothing more than to melt against him and weep for joy, Caro wasn't taking any chances. This man had fooled her twice.

"Didn't you?"

"No. I thought we were in a no-win situation. I thought I was being noble by letting you get on with the rest of your life."

"In other words, you thought it was better to make me feel like an idiot for trusting you, than to explain?"

"At the time, and under the circumstances, yes. I wanted you to hate me so getting over me would be easier. But now everything's different."

"It is?"

"I went back to Frederick because I had a disposable cup with both Rory's fingerprints and DNA on it."

Caro stared at him. "You were investigating Rory?"

"No. Not really. Actually, I think you and I got the same idea at the same time, except I was a little better at getting evidence than you were. I encouraged everybody to take a glass of water at the last class I attended and I grabbed the cup Rory discarded. Then I took it to Pittsburgh and gave it to your sister Sadie to see if she could match Rory's fingerprints to unidentified prints found at a local crime scene. I couldn't investigate because I was too involved in the situation, and also because no one in Wilburn would have answered a question for me. But Sadie was perfect. Close enough that she knew the players and could slip in and out of town and even ask questions, but not so close that anyone suspected she was investigating. And I was right. It turns out Rory is wanted.''

If Max hadn't been holding her, Caro knew she would have collapsed. ''He's a criminal?''

''No, he's just wanted. His fingerprints showed up all over a chop shop in West Virginia. Right now he's being taken in by the state police for questioning, but I have no doubt that once they start investigating they will connect him to a lot more than even I originally suspected.''

''So he's out of Wilburn?''

''For a while. Long enough for Sadie to convince Mary Catherine to establish her reasons for supervised visitation with the court. And once all that happens...''

''Everybody will know Brett isn't your son,'' Caro finished for him, too shocked and too hopeful to voice the next part of her thought aloud.

''Aren't you going to ask me what that means?''

She shook her head. She wouldn't take anything for granted again. From here on out with him, she dealt only in the facts. And as of this minute, a few of those facts remained as they were when he left. "No. You already told me you didn't want to live in Wilburn…"

"I changed my mind."

She stared at him, not quite sure she could believe what she was hearing. "What?"

"I changed my mind. Your sister Sadie convinced me. She's a very smart woman when she's not being a pain in the butt."

"You and Sadie talked?" she asked incredulously.

"Once she had all her investigative questions answered, she started grilling me about other things. And she told me that if I really believed Wilburn needed help so that people like Rory didn't get away with things that I had the skills to help it."

"She did?"

"Yes, she reminded me that with a law degree I could take Pennsylvania's bar exam, get a job in the district attorney's office and take my own personal bite out of crime."

Caro only stared at him.

"No thought on that?"

"I don't know what to say."

"You can say you love me and that you'll marry me."

Caro felt as if her heart stopped. "You want me to marry you?"

"I've asked before. You just have an annoying habit of turning me down."

"I don't know what to say."

"I already told you. Say you love me and that you'll marry me."

Though she wanted to believe every word he said and jump into his arms, she needed a minute to think this through and said the first thing that came into her mind. "Where's Bethany?"

"With my mother. At my grandfather's house... My house. I bought it from my parents for a dollar. The recorder of deeds wouldn't transfer the title without a 'consideration.' So I gave them a dollar and he did it." He shook his head. "Wacky county."

"You've been home for days?"

"Not days. Day. One day to help Sadie tie up a few loose ends."

"And you still want me to marry you?"

"I've only said it three times now."

"Yes!" she said, and threw her arms around him. "Yes! I can't believe this."

"You should be me. In the past two months, I got a baby, found somebody to spend the rest of my life with, and now I'm moving and changing jobs."

She gave him a smacking kiss on the cheek. "I'll help you."

"You'll have to. Not only do I have to study for the bar exam, but I've forgotten so much I'm sure I'll have to take refresher courses."

"We'll do it," she said, then she smiled at him. "I have the feeling we can do absolutely anything together."

"Me, too."

* * * * *

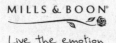

MILLS & BOON®

0406/03b

Live the emotion

_MedicaL
romance™

HER LONGED-FOR FAMILY by *Josie Metcalfe*

Doctor Nick Howell has never forgiven Libby for
running out on him – until she turns up as the new
A&E doctor and it becomes clear that an accident
and resulting amnesia has cut out part of her life.
Now it's up to Nick to help her remember…

*The ffrench Doctors – a family of doctors –
all in the family way*

MISSION: MOUNTAIN RESCUE
by *Amy Andrews*

Army medic Richard Hollingsworth has devoted
his life to saving others. But his medical skills have
put his life in danger – and that of his beloved Holly.
Now, to escape their mountain captors, they must
submit to the bond they once shared…

*24:7 Feel the heat – every hour…every minute…
every heartbeat*

THE GOOD FATHER by *Maggie Kingsley*

Neonatologist Gabriel Dalgleish is passionate about
his tiny patients. It seems as if they are all he cares
for. Except for Maddie. The new medical secretary
slips through Gabriel's defences, right to his
vulnerable heart!

*THE BABY DOCTORS
Making families is their business!*

On sale 5th May 2006